"You mangy mutt, how dare you chase my cats!"

The dog ignored Laura and continued to bark at the cats huddled just out of reach. She grabbed his collar, hoping to distract him.

Sam finally caught up to them. "Don't you hurt him, Laura!"

She tossed her head defiantly. "I'd never hurt an animal. What kind of person do you think I am?"

"You tell me! You're the one who let seven pampered house cats outside. If you want to do that, you'll have to build a fence."

"Why should I put up a fence to keep *your* dogs out?"

Sam gave Laura a look filled with challenge. "It's all part of taking care of the cats. Remember, for the next year those had better be the best-kept cats in South Carolina . . . or you lose everything."

Patricia Knoll, "when facing the imminent arrival of birthday number thirty and baby number four," decided there had to be more to life than changing diapers. She wrote her first Harlequin Romance a few years later. Unlike the heroine of *Cats in the Belfry*, Patricia hasn't always been a cat lover. But her attitude was changed by one amiable kitten who liked children and didn't mind being dressed in doll clothes.

CATS IN
THE BELFRY

Patricia Knoll

Harlequin Books

TORONTO • NEW YORK • LONDON
AMSTERDAM • PARIS • SYDNEY • HAMBURG
STOCKHOLM • ATHENS • TOKYO • MILAN

ISBN 0-373-15451-8

Harlequin Romance EasyRead edition February 1992

This book is dedicated to my sister,
Betty Forsythe,
the living example for every sweet-
natured character I've ever created.

CHAPTER ONE

"WOULD YOU LADIES like some more tea?" Laura Decker held the tiny, Blue Onion-patterned teapot with both small hands and looked inquiringly around the circle of guests gathered at her tea table. One of them was Laura's great-aunt, Belle, her smiling, soft-lined face expressing encouragement for her niece's attempt at proper etiquette. The triangular faces of the other three visitors peeked sullenly from beneath frilly dolls' bonnets. It was quite obvious that Millie, Rosamund and Guinevere, Belle's three cats, would rather have been anywhere than at a tea party.

"Thank you, my dear. That would be lovely," Belle answered. "Though I think your other callers would like a little more milk and a little less tea in their saucers."

Laura tottered on spiky high heels around the damask-covered table and wobbled the pot of lukewarm tea over Belle's miniature china cup. "Well, they can't drink it all," the hostess said with a firm nod of her red-gold curls.

Her big straw hat, weighted down by the prize-winning roses she had picked that morning in her great-aunt's garden, slipped over one eye. As Laura sighed in exasperation and tried to shove the hat back up with her elbow, Belle reached out to take the teapot from her and set it on the table. She smiled warmly. "May I say you look stunning in that outfit, Miss Decker?"

"Yes, you may," Laura answered gravely, tucking her chin against her chest to admire the white organza gown Belle had dug out of a huge trunk in the attic and hitched up with a belt and a fistful of safety pins.

Belle laughed and hugged her tightly. Finding herself squished against a soft, comfortable bosom, Laura snuggled closer and inhaled the scent of Cashmere Bouquet powder that clung to the older woman.

After a few moments, Belle held the child at arm's length and they regarded each other lovingly. Though they were seven and sixty, the years didn't matter because they were kindred spirits.

"You really are lovely," Belle said. "Someday a handsome prince is going to come along and sweep you off your feet."

Laura tilted her head and squinted one eye skeptically. "I don't know any handsome princes."

"Perhaps not now, but you know some nice boys. And they'll grow up to be handsome princes."

The little girl wrinkled her nose. "You mean like Joey Beaman in my class at school? He chews with his mouth open. Yuck!" She looked up, wide-eyed with curiosity. "Did you have a handsome prince?"

Sadness touched Belle's face. "Yes, I did."

"Then where is he? He doesn't live here."

"I did something very silly and another princess got him."

Laura shook her head solemnly. "That wasn't very nice. You should get him back."

"That isn't possible." Belle's eyes clouded with memories. Uneasy with the sorrow on her great-aunt's face, Laura wiggled away.

Sensing her niece's discomfort, Belle pursed her lips and lifted her eyebrows coyly. "Maybe when you grow up, I'll have to help you find your prince. Just don't do anything silly after you meet him."

"What if *he* does something silly?"

"Well, just let him know you won't put up with any nonsense."

Laura wasn't sure what her aunt meant, but it sounded kind of bossy—she liked that.

Millie, Rosamund and Guinevere seemed tired of sitting in their hard little chairs. The three cats slunk onto the table, headed for the pitcher of milk.

Alarmed, Laura made a grab for the teapot. It lurched in her unsteady grip and sloshed lukewarm tea onto Guinevere. The cat yowled, jumped, upset the sugar bowl and shot across the room, her bonnet flopping over her eyes. She stopped to wrestle it off before springing up once again, her claws skittering for traction on the hardwood floor.

Millie and Rosamund immediately followed suit, dashing across the table, scattering sugar, milk and pecan praline cookies in all directions. They flew around the room in a wild game of follow the leader—behind the dollhouse, under the bed, in and out of the toy box and over the chairs.

Laura clapped her hands and shrieked with delight, which caused her heavy headgear to bob, while Belle leapt from her chair and opened the door. The three destructive guests bolted for the stairs.

Shaking her head, Belle surveyed the wrecked table, then turned to her still-giggling niece. "My dear Miss Decker, I believe your tea party is over."

Laura gathered handfuls of organza and performed a wobbly curtsy. "Thank you so much for coming, Miss McCord." She fixed Belle with a stern look. "But next time I'm afraid you'd better come without your friends."

Belle sighed comically, rolling her eyes and shrugging her shoulders. "They don't have very good manners, do they?" She sat down and pulled Laura close once more as the two of them dissolved into laughter.

LAURA DECKER BLINKED, bringing herself out of her memories, then sighed. "I wish we could have had just one more tea party, Aunt Belle."

She glanced around the quiet cemetery. The late-summer air was still and humid, pressing its heat down on her. Droning insects hung, suspended in the air, as if flying away required too much energy.

As the strong scent of roses, stocks and nasturtiums drifted up to taunt her, Laura lifted a small lace handkerchief to catch the tears spilling from her eyes. "This would be easier if you'd been more honest in your letters the last two years. Why didn't you tell me you were sick? I would have been on the first plane home.''

Of course there was no answer.

Laura looked down at the mound of earth covered by an army-green tarpaulin, then over to the yawning mouth of the new grave that scarred the precisely mowed perfection of the wide lawn.

Fresh tears pinched her nose, set her chin quivering and tugged at her heart. She didn't even bother trying to stem the flood that threatened. Instead, she let the tears flow freely, mopping as best she could with the ridiculously inadequate square of linen and tatted lace she always kept in her purse.

Laura gestured with the sopping handkerchief. "You taught me to always carry one of these, you know." She clutched it in her long, slim fingers, swiping at the moisture on her cheeks. Her sherry-gold eyes filled again. "It wasn't easy trying to live up to the ladylike standards of someone who carried calling cards and dressed for dinner, but I tried, and I always have a fresh hanky."

A watery smile touched her lips. "Oh, Aunt Belle. I love you and I'm going to miss you. You remember Jason don't you? Well, we've been thinking about getting married. I wish you could be there. I know I'm breaking one of your cardinal rules—crying over what can't be changed—but you'll have to try to understand.''

A deep sigh forced itself past the lump in her throat. She wouldn't think about Jason Creed, marriage or her new job any more. With a resolute stiffening of her shoulders, she dabbed her red-rimmed eyes, swabbed at her nose and stuffed the hanky back into her purse.

Behind her, two attendants leaned on their shovels as they waited in the shade of a drooping willow to finish their jobs. She knew Belle would have fretted at keeping people from their work, so she turned to walk away.

Laura's steps dragged, but she forced one foot in front of the other and, as Belle had taught her, began searching for the positive. She breathed deeply, in calming gulps, and straightened the belt of her sunny yellow dress. Her tear-softened mouth rueful, she glanced down and fingered the crisp linen. Belle had left specific instructions for her funeral, including the edict that absolutely no one was to wear black. Laura had willingly gone along with Belle's wishes, as had most of the large crowd of mourners. The resulting mix of colors and textures had helped Laura feel hope rather than despair.

The funeral home had offered Laura the use of their chauffeured limousine, but she'd declined. She had wanted a few moments alone, since she had arrived barely in time for the funeral.

Now, as she neared a stand of willows, Laura turned to survey the peaceful, well-kept grounds and then focused once again on her great-aunt's grave. The next time she came here, a gray marble headstone would be in place, the top border elaborately decorated with cats—Belle's companions in life and her guardians in death. And along with Belle's name and the dates of her birth and death would be the epitaph "Life is for living...so get on with it."

She knew all this because the stone had been ordered years ago and stored in Belle's garage until it was needed. When she had first seen the headstone resting against the garage wall, Laura had been frightened by the idea of Belle's death. Her aunt had smiled sympathetically. "Only my body will be gone, honey—" she'd said before tapping Laura's skinny little chest "—but I'll be living right in here."

Comforted by the memory, Laura felt a smile tugging at her lips. She plucked the wrap front of her dress away from her body and fanned some air over her perspiring throat. The climate was actually cooler than what she'd recently left in Senegal, but just as humid. It helped that she kept her strawberry-blond curls in a short, cool style. Still, she needed to get out of the sun.

Anxious to pick up the suitcase she had left at the bus depot and rent a room at Webster's one and only motel, Laura started off again. She headed toward the edge of the cemetery, but stopped with a gasp of alarm when a man stepped from behind the widespread branches of a magnolia tree.

"It's about time you got here," he said in a tone much cooler than the day's temperature.

Laura's gaze shot to his face. "I beg your pardon?"

"You should have arrived days ago—or *weeks* ago."

Confused and offended, Laura drew herself up. She could stare down most people. She'd had plenty of experience as the oldest of six children; not only that, her position as an executive secretary with the State Department had trained her in toughness.

The man before her didn't look intimidated. He looked irritated. And the slight irregularity of his features made him seem somehow disturbing. His nose was large and high-bridged, his mouth straight and grim. Deep-set, icy gray eyes brooded underneath eyebrows that matched his sable-brown hair. Ironically his lashes were long and thin, giving his face an absurd softness, which caught and held her attention for several moments.

Finally she dragged her gaze from his eyes and studied the aggressive jut of his chin, wondering who he was and what he wanted.

"Well, aren't you going to say anything?" he growled, narrowing the gap between them.

Although his size and nearness were slightly menacing, Laura held her ground and regarded him steadily. She was grateful for her height and the two-inch heels that put her level with his six-foot frame. "You seem to know me," she said evenly. "But—"

"Of course, I do. You're Belle's niece." He spread his hands and raised his chin arrogantly. "There are pictures of you all over her house." His hands dropped to his sides, but Laura noticed warily that they opened and closed into fists.

With cool patience she asked, "And you are . . . ?"

"Sam Calhoun."

Laura blinked. This hard-faced stranger was Belle's neighbor? The one who was "such a nice young man"?

"Mr. Calhoun." She nodded, giving away none of her feelings. She was good at hiding her thoughts when she needed to; it was part of her personality, as well as her training. "If you'll excuse me." She started around him, but he moved sideways blocking her path.

"You still haven't answered my question."

Laura tossed her head. "Not now, Mr. Calhoun."

"Yes, now," he said through his teeth, his eyes direct. "I want to know why you couldn't take time from your busy schedule to come see your aunt. She talked about you constantly. Bragged about you. Looked forward to having you come."

Laura's jaw dropped. Her face drained of color until her freckles stood out like beige flagstones on white marble, then flushed angrily. "I was in Senegal. That's in West Africa, halfway around the world!"

"You never earned a vacation?"

"Of course I did. My plans were all made to come and see her, but I—"

His eyes widened in challenge. "What? Got a better offer?"

Laura's hands tightened on her small clutch bag, her short nails scoring little half-moons in the white leather. "I don't owe you an explanation. I don't even know you."

"I know *you*," he said in a deadly tone. "All too well."

"Why, you..." Fury choked her and she fought for control. "You insensitive jerk! I just left my aunt's funeral. I loved Belle."

"So did I. She was my best friend."

Anger gave way to a flash of surprise at the sincerity in his voice. She searched his face trying to identify the emotions underlying his words as she flipped through the mental file she kept of Belle's letters, trying to recall information about him.

"Mad at the world, honey. He's been through a rough time. He just needs a little sympathy and understanding."

As far as Laura was concerned, he needed a muzzle.

It was hard to believe that her kind, gentle great-aunt could have been friends with such a man, but she had to admit he seemed genuinely upset by Belle's death. His face was drawn and tired.

"I know how you must be feeling..." she began in a soothing voice.

"Don't patronize me." He set his feet apart and crossed his arms over his chest belligerently. "I know why you've arrived at such a convenient time, even late for the funeral."

"There was a mix-up—" She broke off. "Besides, I don't owe you an explanation," she repeated huffily, lifting her chin. "Listen, why don't you just get out of my way?" Her eyes raked over him disdainfully. Head up, shoulders straight in a pose that would have been the envy of any monarch, she stepped around him and this time he let her go.

Laura told herself not to get upset. He wasn't worth it. She wished he'd at least been civil, though, because she wanted so much to talk about Belle with someone. But not *him*.

"What a jerk," she muttered again, her long-legged stride carrying her quickly away. She didn't look back, but heard his shoes scrape on the sidewalk. She just hoped he was going in the opposite direction.

"Aunt Belle, you can really pick 'em," Laura murmured, sure that he was one of the dozens of people Belle had tried to help over the years. Her elderly aunt had often succeeded, giving needed encouragement to many who had gone on to straighten out their lives.

Sam Calhoun must have been one of Belle's failures. With a sad shake of her head, Laura paused at the corner, surveying Webster's sleepy main street. The cemetery was at the town's south end, near a white clapboard church that she knew had been built in the

1850s. Main Street's black-topped surface meandered through cottage-dotted hills to join a state highway a few miles distant.

Webster hadn't changed much since the summers she had spent here as a child. The town was located on one of the plateaus of South Carolina's Piedmont area, known to the state's residents as Up Country. It had a genteel quality, a quiet strength and a belief in maintaining its traditions. On summer nights, band concerts and dances were still held in the big gazebo in the town square. The county fair and flower shows were the highlights of the year.

Laura smiled, remembering the first summer she'd been allowed to stay at Belle's. She realized now that it had been so her mother and new stepfather could have a honeymoon without a curious seven-year-old underfoot, but it had established a pattern for all the other summers of her growing-up years. She had made friends in Webster and, in many ways, felt that it was her hometown; because of her stepfather's job with an oil company, the family had moved frequently, never settling anywhere for long.

Laura crossed the street and headed toward the bus depot. She found herself nodding politely to people as she passed, although one part of her brain couldn't believe she was acting so normally, given what had just happened. Also, she felt somewhat resentful that people could go about their business as if it was an ordinary working day. Her mouth tightened. Of course it *was* an ordinary working day. Belle had lived in Webster all her life and raised her sister's orphaned son here, but the death of one citizen, no matter how loved, wasn't a reason to close up shop.

Thinking of how her aunt had been revered made Laura recall that Calhoun man's strange statement about Belle's being his best friend. Laura was still acquainted with a few people in town. Maybe she should ask one of them if it was safe to let Sam out on the streets. The Reverend Mintnor would know about him.

Laura's mouth tightened. At least one good thing had come from the encounter. He had shocked her out of the gripping numbness that had crippled her since the phone call from her mother the night before.

It had taken Marian two days to track Laura down at the apartment she'd just sublet in Washington, D.C. The phone hadn't been connected and Laura had been blissfully moving into her new place, enjoying the peace and quiet after a two-week visit to the crowded family home in Anchorage, Alaska. Laura's brothers and sisters, ranging in age from ten to eighteen, kept the place jumping. Although she had loved seeing them and reveled in the controlled chaos, she'd been glad to be alone again.

The plan had been to move into her apartment this week, visit Aunt Belle next week and then start her new job as an executive assistant to a government under secretary.

Her mother had finally managed to get a call through to her new boss, who had brought the message. All over again, Laura felt the shock and chill that had overwhelmed her.

"Oh, Belle, why couldn't you have waited for me?" she mourned, experiencing a fresh wave of sadness. Reaching up, she rubbed her forehead with the back of her wrist.

Walking along the concrete under the merciless midday sun, she barely noticed what was going on around her, but the noisy rumble of a truck engine caught her attention. Distracted, she glanced over to see a battered old green International pickup keeping pace with her. Sam Calhoun was behind the wheel, craning his neck to see her.

She whipped her head around and walked faster, her long legs stretching out like a Thoroughbred's, her yellow skirt swinging freely between her slim knees, then belling out again.

"Laura, I want to talk to you," he shouted over the engine's throaty rumble. When he shifted the gears they ground out a protest. The vehicle sounded as if it was ready to drop its transmission any second.

"We talked." She sent him a disparaging, don't-waste-my-time look that had always worked with minor bureaucrats at the American embassies in France and Senegal. It bounced off Sam Calhoun like a drop of water off a hot skillet. He just kept driving slowly beside her, holding up traffic.

When she started to step from the sidewalk at the corner across from the bus station, he wrenched the truck in front of her. The truck jerked as he stomped on the emergency brake. His eyes on her, he slid across the seat to open the passenger door with a hefty upward jerk of the handle. His body filled the opening as he stretched toward her. "Get in. I'll take you out to the house."

At his commanding tone, Laura clapped her hands onto her hips. "I'm not going anywhere with you! I know you're upset about Aunt Belle's death, but I won't allow you to harass me! I'm calling Sheriff Blakely!"

"Well, I hope you've got a loud voice. He retired and moved to Florida." Sam leaned forward and braced one hand against the open door. The other gripped the back of the tattered seat. "Hunkle is sheriff now."

Her nose wrinkled. "Farley Hunkle?"

"That's right."

She shook her head in slow wonder. Farley wasn't much older than her own twenty-six years and, as she recalled, had sensitivity that almost equaled Sam's.

She waved a disdainful hand. "Just leave me alone."

Sam's gaze darted to the street ahead, then back to her. His eyes were filled with sincerity and his voice was coaxing. "Look, Laura, we need to talk, and there's something I want to show you at Belle's house. Something you would have seen if you'd come sooner."

Confused and touched by his sudden change in tone, Laura shook her head. He seemed determined to make her feel guilty, and she was just as determined not to let him know she already felt that way. Since receiving the call about Belle, she had been wrestling with remorse and regrets, but Sam Calhoun didn't need to know that.

Still shaking her head, she took an automatic step backward. She tucked her purse under her arm and crossed her hands at her waist. "No. Not now."

He made a guttural sound of quick impatience. "You're going to be staying there, anyway. May as well let me give you a ride."

"No," she repeated. Her curls danced as she shook her head for emphasis. "I'm getting a room at the Webster Inn."

"You can't."

His self-assurance made her steam. "I can't?" she repeated, her golden eyes beginning to fill with challenge. "We'll just see about that."

"The place is being fumigated," he said, jerking his thumb in the general direction of the small motel. "Full to the rafters with termites. You wouldn't want to sleep there. The bed might collapse in a heap of sawdust."

Laura gaped at him in dismayed astonishment. She *couldn't* stay in Aunt Belle's memory-packed house. She wasn't ready to handle it. To her dismay, tears spurted into her eyes again. Turning her face away from Sam, she blinked rapidly, trying to drive them back.

Too much had happened in the last twenty-four hours. She needed time to adjust to it all— or at least to some of it.

The air stirred beside her as Sam jumped out of the truck and came to join her. He took her arm and dipped his head to look into her face. The warm intimacy of his touch jolted her into further confusion. She assumed he was trying a new strategy, because his expression now seemed sympathetic. When he spoke, his voice was gentle with understanding. "Come on, now. You need to get out of this heat. Do you have a suitcase or something?"

This sudden compassion had her scrambling to regain her mental balance. He seemed so strong, so concerned, so overwhelming, that she trembled inside. To calm herself, she pulled away from his disturbing touch and drew a ragged breath. "Yes. It's at the bus station." She lifted a limp hand toward the small building across the street.

He nodded thoughtfully. "Well, I'll bet Eula May has it all ready for you. I'll go get it and then take you on out to the house. You'll see. Everything will be fine."

Laura shook off her perplexity and flashed him a resentful glance, hating him for the kindness, the old-world gentlemanliness that was undermining what little self-control she had. Wearily she let her head droop like a rain-soaked flower on its stalk. She ran her fingertips across her damp forehead. "All right."

With remarkable efficiency, Sam helped her inside the battered truck, slammed the door, then dashed over to the bus station to fetch her suitcase. Laura watched him through the cracked windshield. He returned in less than two minutes, swinging the expensive leather bag she'd purchased in Paris onto the bed of his disreputable old truck. It landed on top of a canvas-covered mound, then tumbled down next to a spare tire. Wincing, she turned around to face the front. Sam opened the door and slid behind the wheel.

He threw her a quick, assessing glance and she straightened automatically. He didn't speak for a minute and Laura wondered if he was trying to find something tactful to say. For someone with his obnoxious personality, that was probably hard to do, and yet, she recalled those moments of kindness.

She kept her voice soft and even, to hide her hurt. "Exactly what is it you think I've done, or failed to do, Mr. Calhoun?" she asked.

Sam wrestled the obstinate gearshift into place and eased up on the clutch as he pulled out into Webster's light traffic. He glanced at her, then straight ahead. "I came on a bit strong back there. Bad timing. My manners need a little polishing."

Laura thought there was a long way to go before that could be considered an apology. "They need a major overhaul," she pointed out bluntly.

He shrugged one shoulder, accepting what she'd said, though apparently not agreeing. "I expected you to come see Belle long before now." The statement was bald, establishing the battle line between them. He underscored his challenge with a narrow-eyed glance.

"What right do you have to expect *anything?*" she asked with prickly defensiveness. She fought the urge to fly into explanations. He wouldn't listen, and she preferred to keep her guilty regrets to herself, anyway.

"The right of a concerned friend," he shot back.

"As I said, there was a mix-up," she enunciated in the ultrapolite tone she reserved for annoying shop clerks and rude American tourists who had stormed the embassy regularly and insisted she do something about their outrageous hotel bills. "Someone contacted my mother in Alaska, but she had a hard time finding me."

"*I* called your mother." Muscles flexed in his arm as he slowed and shifted gears.

"Oh...well, thank you," she said, with a stiff nod. She gazed out at the small town, counted the oak trees that stretched into the distance and tried to sink back into the numbness that had carried her this far. Her eyes were dry now, but she knew she probably still looked shell-shocked. What she needed was time to heal, to think, to decide what must be done next.

Sam apparently had no intention of allowing her any such considerateness. His glance touched on her, then returned to the street. "What I said earlier was true. Belle was my best friend."

Laura looked over at him sharply as they bounced around a corner and started down the street that led to the old house. She didn't know why he'd said that unless he was trying to justify his actions. If what he said was true, there were things he could tell her about Belle that she ached to know. She'd heard that her great-aunt had died peacefully in her sleep, but that was the only thing she knew. It galled her to ask for information from a know-it-all like Sam Calhoun, but she would do it.

Her thumbs played with the clasp on her handbag. "Had she been ill very long?" If so, why hadn't Belle let her know? The void left by Belle's passing throbbed with loneliness.

"Not at all. She was involved in her work with the new library. In fact, she was the moving force behind the project." Sam slowed for a school zone, absently watching the children who straggled across in front of the truck. "I was over there every day."

A flag of alarm raised itself in Laura's mind. She turned on him. Color washed into her cheeks and incredulity filled her eyes. She leaned forward, all but shaking with her roiling emotions. "Well, if you were her best friend, couldn't you have made her slow down? Couldn't you have helped her organize the library project? If you were her *best friend,* couldn't you have done more for her?"

CHAPTER TWO

HIS HEAD SNAPPED AROUND. For the first time, Laura recognized grief that matched her own lining his face. "I did everything she'd let me do," he said with savage emphasis. "And she was never really ill."

Some of her distress eased at that knowledge. "I thought she'd been sick and just hadn't told me."

"Would you have come to see her if she had?"

So much for understanding! If her glance had been a shotgun, he would have been picking buckshot out of his behind for a week. "Listen here, mister—"

"Here we are," Sam said, ignoring her and pulling into the rutted drive that curved in front of the old Victorian-style house.

Laura looked at the building then shifted uncomfortably. Dread settled onto her chest like a ten-pound brick. "I've changed my mind. I can't go in there." She hated the quaver in her voice, but couldn't control it.

Sam braked to a stop before the front steps and cut the engine. He waited, his wrists resting on top of the steering wheel, his hands clenched. "There's something I know she wanted you to see."

Laura turned anguished eyes to him. "Can't you bring it out here?"

Some of the hardness left Sam's face. "I'm afraid not."

Her back straightened. She didn't want to show weakness in front of this man. Somehow it seemed very important that she be strong. Finally she nodded with a quick jerk of her head. "All right."

"Good girl," he said gently, and climbed out of the truck, slamming the door behind him.

Laura blinked at the soft approval in his voice and wondered why she felt gratitude shivering to life inside her. She didn't need any warm feelings for him—things were confusing enough. But darn it, these flashes of kindness threw her off balance, leaving her with a crazy awareness of his rugged good looks, his masculinity. Impatiently she tried to open the door, but the handle wouldn't budge. Remembering the yank Sam had given it earlier, she tried again, her lips firm with determination. It still stuck. She glanced up, frustrated.

With an apologetic shrug, Sam opened it for her from the outside and said, "Sorry. I should have warned you it doesn't open easily from the inside."

Laura gave him a slightly amazed look as she slid from the truck. Why did he drive this bucket of bolts, anyway?

As if he could read her thoughts, humor sprang to life in his eyes, warming the gray. Laura felt herself responding to the hint of boyishness when he said, "Hey, it runs."

When he slammed the door, the noise started off a round of barking among the neighborhood dogs. Laura, still flustered by her odd reaction to him, turned away and looked up at Belle's house, surprised that some of the anxiety had begun to abate. The last time she'd visited, just before her assignment to France three years ago, the house had been sliding into disrepair. The paint had been peeling and a couple of the shutters had drooped forlornly by one hinge.

Now it was freshly painted in a pale yellow, and the trim was a darker shade, closer to goldenrod. The porch railings and glass-paned front door were done in Belle's favorite color, an eye-catching blue. Laura smiled, pleasantly surprised by the improvements.

She tilted her head back to see the turret room on the north side of the house. The windows' diamond-shaped panes glinted in the afternoon light, welcoming her to her old bedroom.

Free of dread and strangely excited, she faced the porch. A faint smile curved her lips as she anticipated the inside of the house. Belle had always said she kept busy with committees and volunteer work so she wouldn't have to stay home and deal with housecleaning. Laura had often urged her to hire help, but the old woman had refused, saying she liked things the way they were. She knew just which pile of clutter to search through for whatever she needed.

Laura climbed the steps and waited while Sam pulled a key from his pocket and unlocked the door.

He pushed it open and gave her a swift glance, as if checking to see how she was handling things. The smells that swept out immediately flooded Laura with memories. Beeswax polish. Dried flowers. Dust. Cat boxes.

Inside, everything was just the same. The furniture was a mix of valuable antiques and cheap imitations, but every single piece gave off an aura of having been loved and used for years. The floors were hardwood, long unpolished, with an edging of grime in the corners. A braided rug that didn't match anything else in the room lay on the floor before the camelback sofa.

Home. The word and the feeling of being where she belonged drifted into Laura's mind. It was ridiculous, of course. She knew the house hadn't been left to her. Belle had told her years ago about the trust fund set up for the cats. The house would be sold to provide for them.

The cats. Laura surveyed the room, puzzled that there weren't two or three of the creatures twining around her feet. Alarmed, she looked at Sam, who had been patiently waiting while she got her mental bearings. "Where are—?"

"The cats? That's what I wanted to show you. This way." He pointed toward the back of the house.

"Who's been taking care of them?"

"I have."

Laura walked through the dining room with the beautiful cherrywood table and sideboard that had belonged to her great-great-grandmother and was the only remnant of the wealth that had distinguished the McCord family before the Civil War. She glanced up. Sure enough, the ceiling was still stained from the time she had let the bathwater run over when she was nine.

In the kitchen she noticed that some of the cupboard doors had been stripped of their layers of ancient paint and awaited refinishing. She wanted to pause and ask about the work in progress, but Sam pointed again and she realized that he was indicating the back porch. She frowned. Previously the cats had enjoyed the run of the house. Were they confined now to the drafty porch? Belle wouldn't have liked her precious pets treated this way.

Her eyes flashed with anger but she bit back her words and opened the door, then started in surprise. The porch had been transformed into a sun-room. Cats lounged on chairs and sofas, behind tables and on windowsills. The windows, shades, paint, even the furniture, were new.

Laura looked at the fat, lazy cats, a half dozen or more, some of whom were bestirring themselves to come and rub seductively around her and Sam's ankles. A bubble of hysteria rose in her throat, followed by another and another.

"I don't believe this," she choked out on a hiccup of laughter. "Why, this is beautiful." She shook her head in wonder, her eyes brimming. "Before I opened the door, I thought—"

"That these pampered babies were being mistreated?"

"Well, yes."

Sam was standing behind her, and when she glanced around, his eyes narrowed slightly as he took in the delight on her face. "She had this room built just for them, but they let her join them. She used to sit in here in the evenings, reading to them, talking..."

Laura saw his craggy features soften. His grey eyes warmed with amusement once again, and his thick-lashed lids drooped lazily. As she watched, his mouth shifted. One corner came up while the other tilted downward. He had a crooked smile. Of course. It couldn't have been any other way. His features were too pleasantly irregular to be marred by a perfect smile. The only thing perfect about his face were those incredible eyelashes.

Jolted by the direction of her thoughts, Laura looked away in confusion. She ducked her head to inspect the cat at her feet. "Oh, Percival!" she cried. "You're still here."

She scooped him up and looked around for any other familiar faces. "Oh, and there's Guinevere."

Carrying the long-haired white Persian, she walked over to sit down beside the pet that had always been her favorite. She was the third female cat that had carried the name and was close to her tenth year. Laura ran her hand down Guinevere's back and was rewarded with a haughty glare. "You fat old thing," she murmured. "Don't you know old ladies like you have to watch their weight?" The regal feline arched her back in acceptance of Laura's touch.

Sitting on the sunny window seat, with its yellow-striped canvas cushions, she started to count. "Seven?" she asked Sam in surprise. "When did Aunt Belle get so many?"

Negligently he shrugged one shoulder. "The last year or so. She never could turn away a stray, and there seems to have been an explosion in the cat population around here." He crouched to carefully lift a gray, tiger-striped tabby and cradle it against his chest. "This is Millie," he said, by way of introduction. "And the others are Belinda, Lancelot, Cyrano, and Rosamund." His smile was fleeting. "Belle always had a classical bent and she liked to use the same pet names over and over." He glanced up. "She didn't tell you about her new friends?" His tone was casual, but the expression in his eyes was not.

Laura didn't bother to keep the swift rush of impatience from her voice. "No. It appears there are a number of things she didn't tell me."

He didn't seem to believe her, but Laura didn't care. She busied herself crooning to the two cats, the only two familiar ones in the bunch. Their coats looked sleek and well cared for. She couldn't fault Sam Calhoun there.

Sam set the tabby back on the floor and walked toward her. Rustling in his inside jacket pocket, he pulled out an envelope. Handing it to her, he said, "I had another reason for bringing you straight here from the cemetery. I had instructions from Belle. She gave me this some months ago."

Puzzled, Laura stared down at her own name, written in Belle's perfect, round, Palmer method penmanship. "What is it?"

He shrugged once more. "Read it and find out."

Laura let him slip the slim white envelope into her hand. Again, she looked at her name, then turned the letter over and examined the back. The edges were frayed, slightly soiled, as if it had been written and sealed a long time ago. Alarm sprinted across her face. "You don't think she knew she was—?"

"No! At least, I don't think so." Sam stepped away, swept back the sides of his jacket and shoved his hands into the pockets of his slacks. "She was just making sure everything was in order. Although it seems pretty funny that you never—''

He broke off and a low rumble of disgust rattled in his throat. ''Never mind. Just read it.''

Irritated that he'd been about to criticize her again for something he knew nothing about, Laura scooted around on the window seat, presenting her back to him. She slid her fingernail under the envelope's flap and ripped it open. Inside was a single sheet of notebook paper, its three holes ragged, as if it had been torn out of a schoolchild's binder. The familiar carelessness brought fresh tears to her eyes. Laura blinked them back as she tried to focus on the words.

''My darling Laura,'' it began, ''I'm giving this letter to Sam Calhoun because I know he'll do whatever is necessary to deliver it.'' Laura glanced up at him swiftly, thinking that he'd delivered it all right, making himself as obnoxious as possible in the process! She tamped down her animosity and went back to the letter.

''If you're reading this, it's because I'm gone. I hope you're not trying to change what can't be changed or sitting there crying. Well, all right, you can cry a little, but then you must get on with your life. I hope you are agreeable to the arrangements I've made in that area, which you'll learn about soon."

Laura frowned. "Arrangements?"

He didn't answer, regarding her with hooded eyes that told her nothing. She returned to the letter.

"I think I know how you're feeling right now, Laura. I've lost many people in my life, including my only sister's only son, whom I had raised. If you hadn't been born before your father went to Vietnam, I don't know what I would have done. You have been one of the greatest joys of my life and I've always considered you one of my best friends, as well."

Laura's hands started to shake, her eyes so filled with tears she couldn't go on. Swallowing the lump in her throat, she fumbled in her purse for her already soaked handkerchief.

Her own feelings matched Belle's. She'd not only lost someone who had loved her unconditionally, but also the one person in the world of whom she could ask anything. To whom she could say anything. Belle had always accepted her individuality. A sudden overwhelming sense of loss swamped her.

AFTER A FEW MOMENTS, Laura felt something nudge her arm and, thinking it was one of the cats, reached over to pull it close to her. Instead, Sam handed her a fistful of paper towels. Gratefully she used them to mop up, but it still took her several minutes to regain control. Finally she took one last swipe at her eyes and resolutely finished Belle's letter, a few more lines of farewell, and then Belle's distinctively beautiful signature.

With trembling fingers, Laura folded the notepaper and slipped it gingerly back into its envelope. As soon as she returned to Washington, she would put it in the safe-deposit box in her new bank. Reverently she tucked the letter into her purse and turned to look at Sam. He was leaning against the kitchen doorjamb stroking Percival, who rumbled approval low in his throat.

The expression on Sam's face made her wonder if she'd just done something to surprise him. His lashes lowered over the speculative look in his eyes.

"Thank you for saving that for me. I'll...I'll always treasure it." Her golden-brown eyes brimmed with more tears. "But couldn't you have given it to me at the cemetery? Why did we have to come back here?"

His shoulders lifted slightly. "Would you have wanted to break down like that in public?"

Laura couldn't meet his gaze. "Well, no."

Sam bent his lanky body to place Percival on the floor, then ambled over to her. "I wanted to talk to you in private about something else."

"What?"

"Do you know anything about the new town library?"

"I know Belle was chairman of the finance committee. She wrote me about it." She felt vindicated that there was at least one thing she could say her aunt had told her.

"The library's finished and the dedication ceremonies are tonight. The people of Webster are grateful to Belle for all she's done..." He paused and his throat worked for a moment. His gaze slid away from her, then back. Laura felt a surge of sympathy as he cleared his throat and resumed. "...all she *did* to see this project through. They had a plaque made up to present to her. You need to come and be the one to accept it."

"Tonight?" she asked on a soft note of dismay. Her aunt had just been buried and he expected her to go to what amounted to a party? No. It was too cold-blooded. She couldn't do it.

He stepped forward to tower over her.

"What's the matter? You don't have to go back to Washington tonight or you wouldn't have been planning to stay at the motel."

She stood to meet him on his own level. "No. I simply think it's crass to have a party when someone's just died."

"It's been planned for weeks. Belle would have wanted it to go on. What did you expect them to do? Put it off until a time that's better for you?"

Her hands clenched. She wanted to yell that she couldn't face any strangers right now. But she didn't. Instead she stared at him coolly. "Since it's for Belle, I'll do it."

He gave her a narrow look, as if he'd expected her to go on arguing indefinitely. Then he sighed. "Oh, hell. I know this is the worst possible time, but no one knew Belle would... Suspected she... The timing can't be helped," he finished, smacking his right fist into his left palm.

Witnessing his distress, Laura felt as if she had stumbled on a private moment of grief. Her mouth trembled open, but nothing came out.

Within moments, he appeared to have shaken off his melancholy. "It's at seven o'clock at the new library," he told her briskly.

"I'll pick you up." Then he swung away and started across the room.

"That isn't necessary."

One of his eyebrows rose. "Oh, do you have a car?"

All her sympathy fled. "Don't be obtuse, Mr. Calhoun. You know I don't. I simply choose to go alone."

"Belle wouldn't have liked that," he said in an unperturbed voice. "She specifically told me to watch out for you."

Her lips thinned. "I can't imagine why. She knew I'm an adult. I've traveled all around the world by myself. There is no need for you to pick me up."

"Don't worry, Laura. Going with me to the library dedication doesn't constitute a long-term commitment on your part."

"And what exactly is that supposed to mean?" An angry flush crept up her face.

He sauntered back toward her, but she noticed his shoulders were stiff. "It means as soon as the amenities are observed, you can go—if you want to."

Laura drew herself up, grateful again for her height and the heels that put her level with his icy gray eyes. She had dealt with irritating men on three continents and in two languages. This truck-driving oaf needed to be brought down to size. "Mr. Calhoun, you know nothing about me. You have no right to talk to me this way. I'm grieving for my aunt. If you're too insensitive to know that, it's your problem." She tried to make her voice cool, but it wavered dangerously.

Sam met her gaze with a challenge of his own, his face as cold as she hoped hers was. "You're probably right. It's my problem." He turned away smoothly. "I'll bring your suitcase in."

He disappeared down the hall, leaving Laura grinding her teeth in frustration. She followed him into the kitchen, being careful to close the sun-room door behind her. Its inhabitants made a few mewing protests, then returned to their naps.

Sam was back a few minutes later. He deposited her bag at the foot of the stairs and gave her a critical look. "I'll pick you up in time for the ceremony." He stalked out the door, and in a meaningless gesture of defiance, Laura hurried over and locked it behind him.

She listened to his truck pull away. It didn't go far. Just a few dozen feet up the road where it turned into another driveway. The barking she had heard earlier started up again, then ceased abruptly. Wondering vaguely when so many dogs had moved into the neighborhood, Laura went into the living room and peeked through the yellowed, dusty lace curtains to see Sam stop in front of a house that had been an abandoned wreck during her childhood. He got out, removed his jacket, laid it on the open truck door and strode around to throw the canvas tarp aside and lift a large sack from the truck bed. With unwilling admiration, Laura watched the ease with which he hefted it onto his shoulder, then walked around the side of the house.

Once he was out of sight, Laura's gaze returned to his house and she grudgingly admired the renovations. If he'd done the work himself, he was a far better carpenter than a diplomat.

The curtain fell back into place as she left the window. She didn't want to ride with him to the library dedication. She was tempted to see if she could get Webster's one and only taxi to pick her up, but unless things had changed drastically, the man who ran it, Tully Cole, was probably off fishing somewhere.

It would have been much easier if she'd rented a car in Washington, but lacking any reliable sense of direction, she probably would have ended up in Georgia instead of South Carolina. Last night it had been easier to hop on the first bus out of Washington and let kindly drivers and ticket agents point her to the proper connections. At least she'd made it in time—barely.

Laura slowly surveyed the cluttered, homey room. As Belle's sole relative she would probably be the one who'd have to sort through the house and sell everything. Her heart clenched at the thought of the unhappy task. Nothing she had faced in her life had been quite as hard as this, and there was no one to share it with her.

She needed somebody to talk to—somebody like Jason Creed.

She and Jason had first met when they were both assigned to the embassy in Paris. The two homesick Americans, both products of small towns, had come to depend on each other in the fast-paced, cosmopolitan city. Together, they had made the rounds of the museums, galleries and concerts, exploring their common interests.

He had also given her career advice and avidly discussed State Department and embassy politics with her. Because their goals and concerns were so similar, their friendship had strengthened. They spent so much time with one another that they'd began to talk vaguely about marriage. Such talk had been tentative since so many miles would be separating them for the next few years. He was staying in Dakar while she was returning to the States.

Laura took a deep, regretful breath at the irony of her situation. She had come back to be near Belle. Now all she had left were Belle's belongings.

She shivered, glancing around the room. Tomorrow would be soon enough to deal with all this. She couldn't think about it now.

Her shoulders drooped wearily. Rest was what she needed. Part of her was reluctant to enter her old room, but a larger part was eager to see if it was just the same, with the flowered curtains and spread she and Belle had picked out years before, and the four-poster bed that had belonged to her grandparents.

In spite of the welter of emotions pulling at her, Laura smiled. Facing this house was certainly preferable to dealing with Sam Calhoun!

Resolutely she left the living room, picked up her suitcase and climbed the stairs to the turret room. In the doorway, she stopped to catch her breath and inhaled a lungful of a familiar scent. She looked around, blinking in surprise, half expecting her aunt to appear. The scent was Cashmere Bouquet, the bath powder Belle had always used. It seemed to rest on the air. Scanning the room, she spied an open box of it on the dresser. Memories washed over her in a wave of longing. But instead of depressing her, Belle's favorite scent—and the recollections it evoked—buoyed her as she continued into her own private aerie.

CHAPTER THREE

As PROMISED, Sam came for her that evening, driving a gorgeous red Thunderbird. He was wearing a soft, oatmeal-colored, linen sport jacket that fit like an old friend.

In her job, Laura saw some of the finest in men's clothing and she recognized this jacket as the work of an expert tailor, though it obviously wasn't new.

This small evidence of his life before coming to Webster made her step back mentally and reconsider him. He possessed an air of competent authority that must have been bred in the bone, as well as a single-mindedness that could be daunting. Altogether, a disturbing man.

And the car! Laura hesitated before sliding in, mentally comparing the plush red interior of the sporty vehicle with the rattling beast he'd driven that afternoon. Obviously there was more to Sam Calhoun than met the eye. Pondering that, she got in and rode through town in virtual silence.

As they neared the new library, Laura leaned forward eagerly, and her breath caught. It was beautiful. Although the building was plain and functional, the designer had managed to make it appealing, with big windows on the north side and a garden with a fountain, flowering shrubs and seedling trees.

The parking lot was jammed with cars and trucks. People of all ages streamed into the building. Sam parked the car, helped her out, and the two of them joined the crowd entering the library.

Once inside, Laura gazed solemnly around, taking in the solid oak bookcases full of carefully arranged volumes, the long tables and the private study carrels. There was even a separate room with small tables and chairs, extrathick carpeting and bright, fat pillows where children could read comfortably.

Sam urged her past people seated in folding chairs toward a row of seats behind the podium. Reluctance dragged at her, but she knew she had to accept the plaque and make a little speech. Three years of handling crises at the embassies had taught her to think on her feet, but now she couldn't seem to decide what she should say.

The two of them sat, and within a few minutes, the mayor called for quiet. After a mercifully short speech, he introduced the head librarian, who came forward with a large, engraved plaque.

Nervously Laura stood and accepted the memorial. She watched familiar faces blur through the tears in her eyes. "On behalf of my aunt, I want to thank you. This town meant everything to her. She would have been humbled and honored to receive this."

Clutching the plaque to her chest and turning blindly, she found her seat. As the applause began, she felt a hand reach out to clasp hers. Sam was looking at her with a flicker of approval on his face. A confusing mix of gratitude and pleasure filled her as his hand tightened once, then fell away.

Even though she knew what he thought of her, Laura felt comforted by his gesture. She saw it for what it was—support given on behalf of his friendship with Belle—and accepted it as such.

When the speeches were finished, refreshments were served. Laura wandered around with a cup of punch in her hand, speaking to people she knew. Everywhere there was praise for the new facility and the woman whose efforts had made it possible. Laura felt a rush of love and pride that Belle could have commanded so much respect.

As the evening wore on, Laura felt more and more glad that she'd come. Listening to reminiscences about Belle helped her recall the wonderful times she and her aunt had spent together. She also remembered Belle's insistence on living in the present. The past was gone and the future would take care of itself.

Along with the number of people who wanted to talk about Belle, many approached her to sing Sam Calhoun's praises.

"Him moving in next door to Belle two years ago was the best thing that could have happened," Mr. Sweeting, one of her aunt's neighbors, told her. "We weren't sure if he'd fit in at first, him being from New York City and all, but it worked out fine. He's been a big help to Belle and a real asset to the community."

New York? Oh, yes, Belle had mentioned that in one of her letters. Laura thought of Sam's old truck and the sports jacket that had seen better days, then of the shiny Thunderbird. They all added to the puzzle that made up Sam Calhoun. After a few moments, Mr Sweeting was called away and the Reverend Mintnor strolled up.

"I can't tell you how glad we all were when Sam started looking out for your aunt," he said, nodding over his glass of punch. "He would do anything for her."

"I'll bet," Laura murmured, curving her lips into a polite smile. She felt defensive, as if people were silently condemning her for not being around for Belle—just as Sam did. And just as she did in her deepest moments of regret.

After a few more minutes of conversation, the Reverend Mintnor ambled over to the cake table. Laura let her eyes search the room for the object of everyone's affection. Sam was near one of the open windows, talking to an enthralled group of women and girls. They all seemed to lean forward simultaneously to catch what he was saying, then they broke apart, laughing at the punch line of his story.

He laughed, too, throwing his head back so that the long curve of his throat was revealed. When his chin lowered again, he was still smiling crookedly. He glanced over to see Laura watching him. With a nod, he excused himself and came straight toward her, though he was detained a couple of times along the way when someone put a hand on his arm to talk to him.

Laura noted the intent way he listened, as if the person speaking was the most important one he'd heard all evening. She felt a moment of regret that he didn't listen to her like that. He had a great many preconceived ideas about her. She was still unsettled by the rude way he had approached her that afternoon. But he had given her time to adjust to entering Belle's house, and he had seemed to understand how hard it was for her to accept the award in her aunt's honor.

He finally reached her, gave her a probing look and said, "I'll take you home. You're probably ready to drop, although this party must seem pretty tame compared to what you're used to."

Laura's forgiving thoughts scattered on a burst of irritation. Her head lifted and her eyes darkened as she answered, "You know nothing about me, and you prove it every time you open your mouth."

His eyes were icy gray as he watched her. "I know enough."

He stretched out a lean, strong hand, but she prevented him from taking her elbow by tucking it tightly against her side. Together, they said their good-nights and Laura again thanked the librarian for the plaque.

Outside, she was ready to step into Sam's car when a short, bald man, perspiring in the night's lingering heat, hurried up to her. "Miss Decker," he called, holding out his hand. "I'm

Harold Pine, your aunt's attorney. If you're available tomorrow, I'd like to go over the terms of her will with you.''

Laura blinked in surprise, glancing from him to Sam and back. ''Terms? Why? I thought everything was set up.''

''It is,'' he agreed quickly, as if he was afraid she was going to raise objections. He whipped a snowy handkerchief from his pocket and mopped his forehead. ''But you need to know about the, uh—'' he looked briefly at Sam before continuing ''—specific arrangements.''

Confused, she suddenly remembered that word from the note Belle had left with Sam. ''Will these 'arrangements' take more than a week or two? I have to start my new job soon.''

Sam harrumphed low in his throat.

Laura threw him a scathing glance, tempted to defend herself. She resisted, because after this was settled she'd never see him again, thank goodness! Instead, she told the attorney she would come to his office the next morning.

''I'll drive you there,'' Sam said as they climbed into his car and started toward home.

''No, thank you,'' she answered primly, folding her hands in her lap. ''I'll call Tully's cab.''

''Forget it. He's not available.''

''And why not?''

"His brother just bought the Webster Inn. Tully's helping with the fumigating."

Laura set her teeth in frustration. "Then I'll walk to Mr. Pine's office."

"It's three miles from the house, and it's supposed to be hotter tomorrow than it was today."

Before she could think of another means of transportation, he said, "If you won't let me drive you, why don't you take my truck?"

"Considering your opinion of me, I'm surprised you don't want to come to the attorney's office," she said with a stinging tone in her voice.

"Uh-uh." He shook his head. "This is something I think you'd rather do on your own."

Surprised and pleased by this rare moment of compassion, Laura didn't know quite what to say. "Well..."

"Take the truck," he urged. "I'd offer the car—" he tapped the steering wheel "—but I've got an early appointment to get it waxed."

She'd been staring straight ahead, but now turned slowly and looked at him. "You have to make an appointment to get your car waxed?"

"Sure." Sam caressed the steering wheel as if it were a lover's shoulder. "A guy out at the edge of town does detailing—you know, cleaning it inside and out. No dust ball unturned. Only does two cars a day. Takes weeks to get an appointment with him because everybody in these parts likes his work.''

''I see.'' Watching his long, supple fingers stroke the wheel, she shivered, then dragged her attention away. She stared out the windshield again. This man drove an old truck that was an auto wrecker's dream. Somehow he hadn't seemed the type to worry about having a perfect car.

Sam slanted her a glance as if he had read her thoughts. ''Hey, my brothers are coming in a couple of weeks,'' he mumbled.

An answering smile glimmered on her lips. ''And a guy has to think of his image, right?''

''Right.''

Laura struggled not to like him, not to respond to that hint of charm. He had said infuriating things and was cursed with a judgmental manner. But she was the oldest of six, and sibling rivalry was something she understood all too well.

When they stopped in front of Belle's, Sam didn't get out right away to open the door for Laura. Instead he sat there, apparently studying the house. ''You can sleep over at my place if it'll bother you to stay here.''

Laura uncrossed her long, slim legs and twisted toward him. "You've got to be kidding."

In the reflected porch light he looked cynically amused. "Don't worry, Laura. I don't have any designs on your...virtue."

The way he dropped his voice on the last word sent a ridiculous tingle up her spine. She shifted against the upholstery to scratch away the feeling. "Don't be vulgar, Mr. Calhoun. I simply don't like your attitude. You've criticized and belittled me since we met. I'm glad you considered my aunt your friend, but frankly, I don't know what she saw in you."

He leaned forward, his gray eyes bold, his nose only inches from her face. "Maybe she saw someone who was around when she needed him."

Laura reached behind her for the door handle. "Maybe she saw someone who desperately needed her help in learning how to act like a gentleman!" She jerked the handle. In a swirl of yellow linen, she all but tumbled from the car. "Good night, Mr. Calhoun. On behalf of my family, I want to thank you for everything you did for Belle. That is if you did, indeed, do anything for her. Personally I won't mind if I never see you again."

With that grand pronouncement, she turned and stormed into the house. He didn't call out or try to stop her, and Laura felt quite proud of herself until she remembered she was supposed to borrow his truck the next day. Her heart nose-dived into her stomach. So much for not seeing him again.

She locked the front door and leaned against it wearily as she closed her eyes and tried to empty her mind of the day's unpleasant events. She ruthlessly shoved aside thoughts of Sam and concentrated on the good things that had happened. Although she still felt regretful and lonely, a warm, comforting glow lingered from the library celebration.

Pushing away from the door, Laura headed toward the sun-room. She'd spend some time with the cats before going to bed. They were surely missing Belle and probably needed fresh food and water, not to mention clean litter. Yuck! She would do the cleaning, though, partly because keeping the cats clean was the right thing to do, but mostly so Sam Calhoun wouldn't have anything to reproach her for.

WHEN SHE CAME DOWNSTAIRS the next morning dressed in a green and yellow-flowered sundress, she found the key to Sam's truck on the kitchen table. It made her uncomfortable to think he'd been in the house while she was upstairs, probably in the shower, but she shrugged it off. After all, he was the one looking after the cats. It gave her a warmly smug feeling to know there had been nothing for him to do, since she had taken care of everything the night before.

She ate a breakfast of coffee and toast made from slightly stale bread. Tears threatened again when she thought of Belle buying that bread, expecting to eventually eat the whole loaf herself, but she fought them down, remembering how peaceful and right it had felt to sleep in the turret room again.

Just before eleven o'clock, she went out front to find that Sam had parked the truck in the driveway. With firm resolve, she climbed in and examined the well-worn clutch and brake pedals. It had been a long time since she'd driven a vehicle with a standard transmission and stick shift.

Experimentally she slipped in the clutch, which she found was tight. The spring resisted, causing the muscles in her leg to quiver. She put the shift through all its gears to determine which was which; the guide had been worn off the knob by years of use. Once she'd done that, she reached for the ignition.

To her surprise, the truck started up okay, but it drove roughly, and she had to be careful with the brake. The rubber covering was gone, and the pedal was slippery beneath the sole of her handmade Italian sandal.

She arrived at Mr. Pine's office promptly at eleven and was ushered into a room full of glass-fronted bookcases and tasteful antiques. These weren't for show, she suspected, but were the original furnishings of an office opened more than a century before. She had the impression Mr. Pine maintained a warm place in his heart for tradition and permanence.

The attorney smiled a funny, triangular smile and held out a chair for her. At his desk he pulled out a blue-backed folder and donned wire-rimmed glasses.

From the folder he withdrew a small envelope and leaned across his desk to hand it to her. "This is for you."

Laura glanced down and, with a spurt of pleasure, recognized Belle's handwriting. Another letter. She started to rip it open and then paused, remembering how she had reacted the day before. With a swift look at Mr. Pine's patiently waiting face, she tucked it into her purse to be read when she was alone. "Thank you. Please go ahead." She gestured toward the documents on his desk.

After a short flurry of throat-clearing, he read a number of small bequests to charities, then said. "This is the part that concerns you, Miss Decker. Miss McCord left you the bulk of her estate. Considering the careful way she handled the money she had inherited from her father, the stocks and bonds she purchased over the years and the investments she made in various enterprises, it adds up to a tidy sum."

By the time he reached the end of this speech and told her the amount of the inheritance, Laura was sitting forward, her hand clutching her throat, her eyes wide. "She left it to *me*? Why? What about the cats?"

"Oh, they're mentioned. In fact, that's the one stipulation of your inheritance."

"Stipulation?"

"Yes. Miss McCord insisted that in order for you to inherit, you must stay in her house with her cats for a period of one year. After that, you can take the cats with you wherever you go, but you must care for them until they, or their issue, have all died from natural causes." His fingers smoothed his somber tie, then flicked outward as if he had just rid himself of something distasteful.

Stunned, Laura slumped in her chair. "I don't understand. This isn't what she told me. Years ago she said . . ."

Mr. Pine looked at her over the tops of his glasses. "She changed it just recently. Sam Calhoun—"

"What about him?" Laura asked, sitting up straight as alarm bells clanged a warning.

"He's the executor of this will." Mr. Pine smiled suddenly. It was a don't-worry-your-pretty-little-head-about-it smile that she hated instantly. "Probate will take a while, but until it's settled you can go to Sam for any amount of money you need for your household expenses or those of the cats. He has full control of the trust fund, so if you need money, all you have to do is ask."

Her jaw dropped. "I don't understand. Why should I have to go to him?"

"That's how a trust works. Property is signed over to the trust and administered by an executor after the death of the person who set up the trust."

"In this case, Sam Calhoun," she said in a flat voice.

"It was set up months ago. Miss McCord's savings, as well as her stocks and bonds, were put in the name of the trust," he explained. "Her home will still go through probate." Mr. Pine cleared his throat yet again. "I suppose she didn't have it put into the trust, too, because she wanted it to stay in the family a little longer.''

''A year, to be exact,'' Laura said dryly.

''Well, yes. Trusts are excellent plans,'' he added pedantically. ''I advise all my clients to set up trusts.''

''Do you also advise them to have Sam Calhoun administer the trust?''

The lawyer's face pinkened. ''Certainly not! Miss McCord chose him!''

Laura shifted uncomfortably, not sure that was the way things had gone. She hardly knew Sam, but she had firsthand experience of what it was like to be railroaded by him. ''Well, this arrangement—asking Sam for money—just lasts until probate is settled, right?''

''Yes. That will take a year—or longer.''

Laura rose to her feet and stared down at him. ''Do you mean to tell me that if I need my own great-aunt's money to provide for her cats during the next *year,* I have to go to Sam Calhoun—who is not even a member of our family?''

With his ever-present handkerchief, Mr. Pine began mopping his brow, which was perspiring profusely in spite of the air-conditioning. He succeeded only in bringing a high gloss to his hairless dome.

"Now, Miss Decker, don't be upset. Your aunt made this new provision in her will just recently and I assumed she had told you. You were even supposed to receive a copy of the document itself." His eyes darted nervously toward the wood-paneled door, as if he was planning his route of escape. "And . . . and executors often aren't members of the family."

Laura's knees wobbled and bent of their own accord as she wilted into the chair. She propped her elbow on the chair arm and rested her forehead against her fingertips. Several deep breaths helped restore her somewhat. She hated losing her temper. It always left her feeling embarrassed, wrung out and inwardly shaking. Besides, it was totally at odds with her calm, poised self-image. "I never received such a document," she said firmly, then glanced up guardedly. "How long were you my aunt's attorney?"

Mr. Pine's mouth grew pinched in apparent offense. "For over thirty years."

"And you didn't think it was odd that she would give control of her estate to a virtual stranger?"

"Mr. Calhoun was hardly a stranger and she was in full possession of her faculties—"

"She was coerced," Laura stated firmly. And she knew just who had done the coercing. Sam Calhoun, so-called best friend of her aunt.

"Belle McCord brought Sam in with her when she made the changes—"

"Was he twisting her arm?"

Mr. Pine paled. "She made all the arrangements herself. Right here in this office. Sam even tried to talk her out of naming him as her executor."

"I'm sure he did," she scoffed. The argument would have been all for show, no doubt. The thought of her dear, outspoken, stubborn aunt being deceived by a con man's charm drove her to her feet again, ready to storm out and confront Sam. She marched toward the door.

"Wait," the attorney bleated, jumping up hastily. "What do you plan to do?"

"Go talk to Sam Calhoun, of course!" she tossed over her shoulder.

"But the arrangements are all legal and binding. You need to make a decision about staying in the house."

She was almost at the office door when she swung back, hands on her hips. "Why?"

"Because if you decide not to stay, the cats will be destroyed and the money will go to charity."

Horrified, Laura gaped at him. She lifted a shaking hand to steady herself against the door frame. "Now I know for certain that will is a fake. Aunt Belle would never have made any provision for her cats to be destroyed."

Mr. Pine dropped his gaze. "Well, I did think that was a bit odd, considering how much she loved them."

"A bit odd?" Laura threw her hands in the air, turned and stalked out before she said something about the man's ethics, parentage and brainpower that would probably get her sued.

Her mind racing, she rushed out to the truck, hopped onto the seat and stabbed the key into the ignition. What did she know about Sam Calhoun, after all? Absolutely nothing!

As she pulled out into Webster's light traffic, she tried to recall everything Belle had written about Sam since he'd moved in next door two years ago. He seemed mad at the world and had spent his days, often late into the night, working on the run-down place he'd bought. Belle's letters had held numerous references to him, all glowing with respect and admiration. Laura's brow wrinkled as she tried to remember them. According to Belle, Sam had been talking about going into business for himself. Ha! She just bet. Sam had helped Belle clean out her rosebushes and plant petunias. He had driven her to the grocery store every week, and to the veterinarian when Guinevere developed an abscess on her right hind leg.

At the time, Laura had thought the activities were of the typical neighborly variety. Now they took on sinister overtones. She was positive that Sam Calhoun had been ingratiating himself with Belle.

She squirmed when she remembered the hints Belle had included in her letters that Sam might be the right man for Laura. Those suggestions had stopped once Belle met Jason and saw for herself how much he and Laura had in common. Laura wished now that Belle had kept writing about Sam. At least she would have known what the man was up to.

For an instant she wondered if she was acting a little irrational. Mr. Pine had said that being an executor was of no monetary advantage to Sam; still, Laura was sure there was more to the situation than she was seeing. Otherwise why would Sam have been so judgmental and aggressive since their first meeting? He was obviously hiding a guilty conscience! He didn't want her to find out how he had manipulated her aunt.

Laura shifted gears, grinding them almost into dust, and wrestled the awkward old In-

ternational around the corner to her street. She
glared through the cracked windshield, anxious
to get home and confront Sam. If he knew
what was good for him, he'd be there.

Her uncharacteristically violent thoughts left
her heart pounding and her hands clenched
spasmodically on the steering wheel. She
couldn't believe Mr. Pine had stood by and let
this happen.

She slowed for the school zone, shifting the
reluctant gearshift down, holding the tight
clutch with a shaky leg.

Speeding up once she was beyond the school,
she roared right on past Belle's place and ca-
reered into the driveway of the house next door.
Sam's red Thunderbird, shining and beautiful
after its session with the detailer, sat in front
of the house. He had probably just bought the
car, Laura thought furiously and illogically,
and planned to make the payments with money
siphoned from Belle's trust account.

Fine dirt flew up behind the truck and the
tires fought for traction as she wrenched the
wheel. Laura stomped too hard on the brake
and the old behemoth of a truck fishtailed on
the gravel. She tried to compensate by twisting
the steering wheel, but the smooth leather sole
of her sandal slipped off the worn brake pedal

and hit the gas. The truck zoomed ahead and slammed into the rear of the Thunderbird.

The International's heavy cast-alumimum bumper made short work of the Thunderbird's back bumper, trunk and impressive array of taillights. The screeches of metal meeting metal and shattering glass echoed through the neighborhood and ended when both vehicles pushed forward into a gnarled apple tree. Under the force of the impact, the tree bowed. Green apples pummeled the hood, then rolled and bounced away.

Laura rocketed forward, then back, miraculously unhurt, her hands glued to the steering wheel, her eyes wide in horror as she surveyed the damage. She was looking directly down on the compressed remains of the Thunderbird's bright red trunk. The car was wedged flat up against the apple tree that now bent to smack the ground with fruit-laden limbs.

She had wrecked Sam Calhoun's truck and his car. Both! At the same time!

Going limp, she let her feet slide off the clutch and the brake. She hadn't turned off the engine—which now sounded like a garbage disposal with a spoon caught in it—and the truck lurched, belched and died. Laura would have happily followed suit, because she knew she would never, ever, live this down.

An awful silence filled the air, but it was immediately broken by the wild barking of the neighborhood dogs and the sound of Sam's screen door hitting the front of his white frame house. Blearily she looked over to see him standing on his porch with a jar of mayonnaise in one hand and a knife in the other.

CHAPTER FOUR

THE JAR AND KNIFE crashed to the step when Sam dropped them and sprinted over to her. "Laura! Laura, are you all right?" He wrenched the door open with a downward thrust of the handle.

Fighting her way out of shock, she blinked twice and said the first thing that came to mind. "I'm perfectly all right, thank you. Why did you have your car parked there?"

His eyes widened and his jaw dropped. "It's *my* driveway!"

She started to climb out, and in spite of his traumatized state, Sam automatically reached to help her. She waved away his assistance, but when her feet hit the gravel, her knees buckled like a sailor's after a three-day shore leave. He grabbed her arms and she steadied herself against the door, willing some starch into her rubbery legs. "Well, you should have given me more room to stop."

"Ach!" he choked, letting her go as if she'd scorched him and stepping back to survey the damage. "I can't believe this! You wrecked my... You wrecked my truck!" His gaze darted ahead. "*And* my car, and you accuse *me* of not giving you enough room!" He dashed forward to view the remains of his status symbol. His face turned slightly green. From his throat a series of garbled squeaks and grunts erupted as he fought to form words. His arms flapped the air like a wounded bird trying to fly, then he dropped his hands to his head. He clutched his thick sable hair until it stood up in tufts.

"You wrecked them! You wrecked them both!" His face was flushed, his eyes wild.

Laura loosened her sustaining grip on the truck and stumbled over to inspect the damage. When she saw it, she moaned and put a shaking hand against the trunk of the listing apple tree. The front of the car looked as bad as the back, crumpled and crunched.

"This is a nightmare!" Sam's hands flew out again. He looked at her as if she were an apparition from hell. "How did you manage to destroy both of them?"

Laura inhaled a deep breath that did nothing to stop the wild slamming of her heart. "No one can be expected to drive a truck that isn't properly maintained." One part of her mind knew she should be apologizing. This disaster was entirely her fault. But the things coming out of her mouth weren't at all what she meant to say. The numerous shocks of the past two days seemed to have short-circuited her good sense. She'd been taught to handle almost any diplomatic situation, but her classes in international protocol had never covered anything like this!

A tide of red washed into Sam's face. "Not properly maintained? Listen, lady, you obviously don't know how to drive."

"No one could drive this bucket of bolts!"

Sam opened his mouth, then closed it. He shook his head mutely, staring at her as if she was crazy.

She stared back obstinately even as remorse welled up in her. Suddenly stubbornness wavered and collapsed. She buried her face in her hands, just about to crumple into a tearful apology, when the neighbors began emerging from their homes to see what all the commotion was about. She knew many of them and recognized others from Belle's funeral and the library dedication the night before. Sam sent Laura a furious look that said the discussion wasn't over and stormed into the house to call the police and his insurance company.

Until that moment, Laura had been holding up by sheer grit, but dear old Mr. Sweeting saw the whiteness of her face and, clucking sympathetically, came over to lead her home. "There's no reason for you to stay here, Laura, honey. If someone needs to talk to you, they can find you inside. Uh, how did this happen, anyway?"

Her willowy figure towered over him as he supported her to her own front door. She croaked out an incoherent response and followed him in, trying to recall how it *had* happened. Admittedly she was at fault. She hadn't been paying attention to her driving. All the way to the attorney's office she'd been conscious of the stiff clutch and the slick brake pedal, careful to set her feet on them firmly. On the way back home, she'd been too furious to notice anything except the righteous accusations and arguments she planned to heap on Sam Calhoun.

Mr. Sweeting took her into the kitchen and bustled about making her a glass of iced tea. Laura smiled tremulously. Iced tea was the all-purpose nonalcoholic drink in the South, served year-round and expected to soothe, comfort and console. The kindly old man poured it into one of Belle's exquisite Waterford crystal glasses, added a generous amount of sugar and handed it to Laura. Laura drank greedily, and strangely enough, the simple tonic worked. After a while she'd calmed down enough to convince Mr. Sweeting she could be left alone. He went reluctantly, throwing worried looks over his shoulder and murmuring about bad things happening in threes.

Laura gazed after him, her face so pale the freckles stood out like polka dots. She hoped three things were *all* that would go wrong. First Belle's death, then the truth about Sam Calhoun, now wrecking his truck...and his car...and his apple tree. She was going to do her darnedest to make sure life got better from now on.

A young sheriff's deputy came by to take her statement, followed by the insurance man, a dour soul whom she knew would probably raise Sam's insurance rates because of the accident. She cringed with suppressed guilt.

Sam accompanied both men. Standing by the kitchen counter he glowered at her as she talked. She ignored him, but when she had shown the insurance man out the front door, she turned to find Sam standing right behind her.

"Are you okay?" he asked gruffly, reaching up to grip her shoulders.

She tried to pull away, but he held her firmly, his hands warm on her skin where it was unprotected by her sundress.

"No headache?"

"No."

He examined her closely, gray eyes dark with concern. "No double vision or nausea?"

"No," she answered, twisting awkwardly from his grasp. She lurched away in a swirl of green and yellow and backed up against the table. "I...I'm fine." Nervous fingers plucked at the waist of her dress as she stared at him, dismayed at what she had done to his property. Squaring her shoulders, she dragged in a sustaining breath. Well, she decided, she owed him an apology and there would be no better time for it than the present.

Her remorse died quickly, though, when Sam crossed his arms over his chest and said, "Did you do that on purpose?" He angled his head in the general direction of his driveway.

"Of course not."

He snorted. "You were pretty upset with me last night..."

"I wouldn't deliberately destroy your property, no matter how angry I was." Her shock at the terms of Belle's will flared up again, fueled by his accusation. Her body went rigid and she stuck out her chin. "Although I *do* have plenty of reason to be mad, you...you opportunist!''

''What? What are you talking about?''

''Mr. Pine told me the terms of Aunt Belle's will. The only way she would have written such a crazy document was if you coerced her. How did you convince her to make you executor? She was an old woman!'' Furious with herself because of the angry tears welling up, she pinched her lips together.

Sam's look should have incinerated her on the spot. He stepped closer, leading with his own formidable chin. ''I don't know what kind of weird ideas you've cooked up, but my association with Belle was pure friendship. She wanted someone to make sure you had the funds to take care of the cats, and she thought I could be that someone—if you decide to take time off from your high-flying life and meet your responsibilities, that is.''

Laura's hands formed fists. ''Don't you lecture me on my responsibilities, mister. I'll do whatever is necessary to fulfill Belle's wish.''

''Even if it means staying here for a year?''

He had her there, but she wouldn't admit it. She straightened, wishing she was even taller so she could look down her nose at him. ''We'll see about that. I have a job in Washington, you know. I have an apartment. Friends.''

His eyes narrowed. "If you keep those things, you can't keep the cats, and that was Belle's wish."

"They can come with me."

"Seven of them?" he scoffed. "Face it, Laura. The only way you're going to be able to carry out the terms of Belle's will is to do exactly as it says."

"And ask you for money whenever I need it? Never." Her tone was deadly as she bent forward until they were almost nose to nose.

"Is that what this temper tantrum comes down to? Money?"

Insulted, Laura straightened again and her voice was low and lethal. "No. It comes down to a sleaze-ball named Sam Calhoun taking advantage of a defenseless old woman."

Fury sparked in his eyes and she knew she had struck a nerve, but instead of the denials and explanations she would have expected from anyone else, he said, "Is that guilt I hear in your voice? You weren't here when Belle needed you, so you resent anyone else who was? You neglect her shamefully, then think you can rush back here and pick up anything you can get your greedy little hands on!"

Hurt stabbed through her, but she raised her fists and planted them on her waist. "That's an unjust, untrue accusation!"

"Is it? Belle told me how much trouble you had handling money—how many times you were overdrawn at the bank because you subtracted wrong in your checkbook. She never could figure out why a woman who was capable of organizing a reception for a thousand people couldn't keep track of her own money."

The truth of that stung Laura, making her even angrier, this time at Belle, as well as at Sam. What he said was true. She had to force herself to be careful with her money. But how could her beloved aunt have told that to a stranger? "How I handle my money is none of your business."

"It was my business as far as Belle was concerned. She wanted to make sure the cats were provided for. Obviously she felt she could trust you to love them and feed them, but not necessarily to remember to pay the electric bill."

Laura made a low, strangled sound, her pinched face full of hurt. She didn't answer, though, because she realized the argument was getting nowhere. She decided to break it off. "I'm going to another lawyer. It isn't right that you should have control of Belle's estate. You took advantage of her."

In his eyes and expression she could read the things he wanted to say to her, all of them insulting. He restrained himself with obvious effort. "Do what you want, but it won't gain you anything." He turned and started for the door. "In the meantime, if you need money for yourself or for the cats, you know where to find me. All you have to do is ask."

Laura's temper went off like a rocket as he walked out the door and shut it behind him. She rushed forward, yanked the door open and shouted after him, "I'd rather suck pond scum!"

THAT AFTERNOON she had her answer about the legality of Belle's will. She'd called another attorney in Greenville and wangled an appointment. By some miracle, she had managed to get Tully's Taxi to pick her up and deliver her to the bus station. Then, while the big vehicle had lumbered toward the city, she'd tried to make plans. It did no good, though, because she was still too angry with Sam.

Four hours later she was headed back to Webster, leaning her head against the bus window and staring out at the lengthening shadows.

The attorney, whose specialty was wills and trusts, had said nothing could be done short of going to court. He had spouted a great deal of legalese, but it came down to the fact that Belle's wishes should be respected. It would take a great deal of time and trouble to prove that Sam had unduly influenced her.

The attorney had obviously been puzzled by Laura's concerns. Sam was only the executor. He couldn't inherit and his fee for acting as representative of the estate was relatively small. The lawyer wondered why she was making such a fuss.

That was a good question, and during the monotonous bus ride, she had time to come up with an answer. She was making such a fuss because she couldn't stand the thought of going to Sam Calhoun for money. Not only that, but all her carefully laid plans had been scattered before the prevailing winds of her aunt's will.

Laura freely admitted that she was sometimes inflexible. Once she set her mind on something, she persevered until she got it. She didn't like surprises or sudden upsets. In that, she was like Belle, whose house had remained comfortably cluttered because it somehow meant stability.

She nestled her head against the back of the seat, rolled her eyes, then squinted them shut. As she saw it, she had only two alternatives. Either she abided by the terms of the will, or she didn't.

If she stayed, she could care for the cats, something she would enjoy. She hadn't had a pet of her own since she'd left home for college. Certainly there had been no opportunity to have one in Paris or Dakar.

Also, staying would make it possible to give the sorting of Belle's personal possessions the attention the task deserved. There were things she wanted to keep, others her mother or sisters might want. And Belle had many friends who might enjoy a small memento of her.

Laura pinched her bottom lip thoughtfully between a thumb and forefinger. Those were the positives of staying on for a year. The biggest negative was that she would have to give up her job, and she hated to lose it. The position as executive assistant to a government under secretary couldn't be held open for her that long. This post would have been her first at the executive level after five years as a secretary. If she let the job go, it might be years before she got another such offer. And she had worked so hard in her career.

Inheriting Belle's estate wouldn't provide her with a cushion of comfort if she had no job, because she had no intention of using the money for herself. If it came to her, the money would go to help out at home.

Her brother, Todd, and her sister, Amy, both wanted to be doctors. The inheritance could go toward their education and to help them set up practices. Also, there were three younger children at home who deserved the opportunity to go to college, just as she had.

Laura shifted on the seat and glanced out at the gathering darkness. The inheritance would be the perfect solution to her parents' difficulties with financing the younger children's education. For everyone's sake, she should stay.

The only hitch in her rosy little plan was Sam Calhoun. If she stayed with the cats, she would have to go to Sam for money—for everything from cat food to her own food.

That left the other alternative.

She could turn her back on all of it and let the cats be destroyed. Her stomach lurched sickeningly at the thought. There was no way she could allow that. She couldn't understand why Belle had made such a reprehensible provision in her will, and she simply couldn't let it happen.

Coercion was the only reason she could imagine. But why? The lawyer's words came back to her. Why would Sam want control of Belle's estate? Why would he want to see Belle's beloved cats killed?

She sat forward and pulled the back of her sundress away from her perspiring skin. The bus had air-conditioning that fought a valiant but losing battle against South Carolina's heat and humidity. Laura felt drained and exhausted. If only she could talk to Jason about this, it would help her make a sensible decision. The best part of her relationship with Jason was their shared interests and similar backgrounds. He, too, had experienced a somewhat nomadic childhood, moving around with his mother, who worked as a restaurant hostess. Jason knew and shared Laura's need for stability. She considered calling to ask his advice, but then glanced at her watch. It was after midnight in Dakar, and Jason wouldn't appreciate being awakened.

That left the decision squarely on her, where, of course, it had rested all along.

Laura straightened in her seat. She didn't know the answers to her questions, but she would eventually. Even though she felt nonplussed by Belle's will, she'd just have to accept it. However, there were some things she could do. She could set guidelines for her dealings with Sam Calhoun. She would confront him first thing in the morning and tell him exactly how things would be.

THE WHINING BUZZ of a chain saw pulled Laura out of sleep the next morning. She rolled from the big four-poster bed and made a beeline for the window seat. Kneeling on it, she stared down, bleary-eyed, at Sam Calhoun's broad, bare back as he cut the mangled apple tree into logs.

Laura winced and sank onto the padded seat with her heels tucked underneath her. That tree had been there since before she was born and she had knocked it down in seconds. The least she could do was replace it. Her mouth drooped as she realized she'd have to get the money from Sam in order to do so. She found the possibility infinitely depressing.

For a few more minutes, she watched him, grudgingly admiring the way he handled the saw. His movements were clean and easy, with no wasted motions or energy.

She sat with her hands folded loosely against her short, flower-sprigged nightgown and thought about him. Up until now she had considered him the enemy, but what did she really know about him? Everyone in town sang his praises. Belle had obviously admired him enough to make him executor of her will.

But if he had a job, she hadn't seen any evidence of it. He'd been home for the past two days. When she made her dramatic return from Mr. Pine's office, he had been in his kitchen, making himself a sandwich, which indicated he worked nearby, at home, or not at all.

"Mr. Pine's office!" she said on a gasp, spinning around. She'd been so upset by the will and the car wreck that she had forgotten about the second letter from Belle. Her feet smacked against the floor as she jumped up. She tossed clothing and bedding aside until she'd located her purse and pulled out the letter.

With the chain saw whining in the background, she opened the envelope and removed the single sheet of paper. She scanned the top and saw that it was undated, as the previous letter had been. A faint scent of Cashmere Bouquet drifted up to tease her senses.

It read:

My darling Laura,
I hope you're not angry with me over the terms of my will. I know you've always wanted a career. Remember how we used to talk it over when you were a child? I know it's important to you, and I hate asking you to postpone it for a year to look after my cats, but if you stay, you'll inherit everything. And you can do as you want with the money as long as my pets are well cared for. If you don't agree to the provisions in my will, the cats will be put to sleep. It pains me to say this, but

if you don't love them and care for them, who will? I can't stand to think of my little companions being neglected. If you have any problems, just ask Sam. He's a good and kind man. I would have left the cats to him, but that would have been impossible, as I'm sure you understand.

The letter was signed off with love.

Laura went back and read the sentence about Sam's goodness. "In a pig's eye," she muttered, folding the letter away. She couldn't help the sense of being manipulated from beyond the grave. And what was it she was supposed to understand about Sam not taking care of the cats? He'd been doing it for days, and Belle had seemed to trust him completely in every other way.

"Oh, Aunt Belle," she murmured. "I don't understand what you're trying to tell me about Sam Calhoun."

She looked out the window again as she considered the letter. It removed the last of the doubts she'd had about the possibility of Sam's coercing Belle, and it solidified her decision to stay. Her gaze landed on Sam's house.

Leaning closer to the screen, she surveyed his home, paying careful attention to detail for the first time. He had, indeed, fixed it up. She

remembered the small house as sagging forlornly in a yard choked with waist-high weeds.
The property had an attached acre with a
stream running through it where she had played
as a child. Now the house sported a fresh coat
of pale blue paint, new steps with a white,
wrought-iron railing and a yard full of rosebushes that matched her own, or rather,
Belle's, for beauty. If she craned her neck, she
could see the shine of silver chain-link fencing
at the side of the house. Again she heard dogs
barking and wondered if Sam owned one of
the noisy animals.

Determined to tell him her decision immediately, she pushed away from the window seat
and headed for the shower. Within half an
hour, she was downstairs dressed in apricot-
colored seersucker shorts and top, her short
hair brushed back from her face. She ate
breakfast, fed the cats and decided to let them
out for a while. As far as she knew, the lazy
felines hadn't been outside since her arrival.
They were past due for exercise. She held the
back door of the sun-room open and the seven
of them condescended to troop out and explore the hedge-enclosed yard.

When she turned back toward the kitchen,
her gaze fell on the jar of instant iced tea Mr.
Sweeting had left out the day before. Acting

on impulse, she mixed a tall glass and carried it outside.

As she crossed the yard, she found herself admiring the play of muscles in Sam's back and arms. She knew they would be tight and hard to the touch—not that she intended to touch them!

She had to wait until he'd finished cutting one of the branches of unripe fruit from the tree before she could walk around in front of him and get his attention. He started in surprise and turned, the chain saw held aloft. With a flick of his wrist, he switched off the motor. After it had whined into silence, he set it down and examined her with a long, thoughtful stare. "Good morning."

She answered him cautiously and offered him the glass of tea. "I thought you might be thirsty."

With an inquiring lift of his brow, he took the glass and raised it to his mouth. His eyes closed in appreciation of the icy drink, and Laura's widened in unwilling appreciation of him. She felt oddly breathless as she watched him swallow. Her gaze drifted down his throat, over his muscled shoulders and then skimmed the curly dark hairs that swirled across his stomach and disappeared below the waistband of jeans so faded they were almost white. These denims didn't look as if they had been deliberately bleached for fashion's sake. The color had quite simply been worn out of them by hours in the sun and countless cycles through a washer. They fit tightly across his thighs and...

Laura almost gasped aloud as she realized where her gaze had been straying, and she snapped it back up to his face. Sam had drained the glass and was watching her, his gaze hooded by those incredible lashes. Amusement burned in his eyes. Embarrassment burned in hers.

"Thanks," he said, giving back the glass. He bent to pick up the saw again, but Laura reached out a hand to stop him.

"I was wondering if we could talk," she began hurriedly.

He lifted his head. "About what?"

Her hand fluttered toward the splintered tree stump. "This tree for one thing. I want to replace it."

Sunlight glinted on his dark hair as he nodded. "All right. That's only fair since you knocked it down."

He wasn't going to make this easy for her. "Also, I want to ask you some things about my aunt and about why you're her executor."

"I wondered when you'd get back to that," he muttered.

"No time like the present—" She broke off when a cat's yowl and a dog's bark split the morning stillness. Several more cat shrieks followed, joined by the yipping and howling of a dog. The clamor was coming from behind her house.

"What in the . . . ?" Sam abandoned the saw and started to run toward the noise. Laura was right on his heels, her long legs keeping pace with his.

When they reached the wooden gate at the side of her house, they dashed through, letting it slam shut on its own. They skidded to a stop at the sight of the cats being chased around the backyard by a big tan dog, barking wildly. His outsize feet and awkward lope told Laura he was still a puppy, but the cats didn't know or care. From somewhere nearby more dogs began barking, making known their desire to join the ruckus.

"Stop it, you mangy mutt," Laura shouted, taking up the chase. Sam barreled in with shouts of his own, but she ignored him, hoping to reach the dog and pull him back.

The family of felines, led by Percival, formed a lightning blur of gray, black and orange, followed by their barking, running, snapping tormentor. Ears laid back, bodies stretched out, the cats flew to the top of the picnic table, scampered over its painted wooden surface, then raced across the yard and finally up a chinaberry tree.

Laura followed, clearing the picnic table's detached bench like a hurdler—right leg stretched out straight in front, left one bent at the knee. The pup stopped at the tree's base and circled it, head up, eyes alert, still barking uproariously as if he could order the felines down. Laura finally caught up to him and, furious, grabbed his collar with a firm hand. "You miserable mutt, what do you mean coming in here and chasing my cats?" If she'd been capable of rational thought, she would have realized her foolishness in chasing a strange dog around the yard, much less tugging on his collar.

The canine ignored her, anyway, too busy barking at the cats even to be aware of her hold. His eyes rolled and he froze for an instant before he took off again, dragging Laura along. Her feet stumbled and her sneakers slid on the grass.

"Laura, wait," Sam shouted, running beside her.

She gave him an incredulous look as she sailed ahead, as if asking how he thought she *could* wait.

Ahead of them, poor old Guinevere, slower than the others who had already made it up the tree, was slinking along the base of the hedge, obviously hoping to escape the noisy, slobbering intruder.

"Oh, no, you don't!" Laura twisted sideways on the big pup's collar, momentarily distracting him. He lurched and she let him go, then darted ahead to scoop Guinevere up in her arms. The frightened cat tried to scratch her, but Laura was prepared and quickly caught all four feet in a firm grip.

Once she had the old tabby cradled against her, she spun on the dog. It took considerable restraint to keep from throttling him.

Sam must have read the struggle in her face because he lunged forward to grasp the dog's collar. He turned so his body was between her and the animal. "Don't you hurt him, Laura!"

Laura tossed her head defiantly. "Don't be ridiculous, Sam. I would never hurt an animal, no matter how sorely I was tempted. What kind of person do you think I am?"

"You tell me!" His lips thinned as he knelt beside the dog. With one hand he lifted the pup's head and with the other he pushed down on his rump. "Sit," he commanded sharply. He had to repeat it twice before the animal obeyed, going back on his haunches and whimpering as he rolled his eyes at Sam.

Surprised but relieved that the dog had obeyed him, Laura sighed and looked down at the cat in her arms. "Are you all right, old girl?" she murmured, running her hand lightly behind the cat's ears and down her silky back.

"Is she hurt?"

"No."

Sam was still on one knee beside the pup, his hands gently stroking the short, thick fur. He looked up to survey the yard and the cats lounging in the chinaberry tree as if it had been their planned destination all along. "That's the most exercise this bunch has had in ages. I wonder how they got out of the sun-room."

"I let them out, of course."

He jerked his head up, eyes blazing. "You did! That was a stupid stunt."

Affronted, she stared at him. "I beg your pardon. This is their yard. They have every right to be loose in it."

"Belle never let them out."

"I'm not Belle!"

"More's the pity," he muttered, standing to face her.

Furious color washed Laura's skin, blending with her freckles to create angry red blooms on her cheeks. "They should be safe here from strays and what's more, I—"

"He's not a stray. He's mine."

"Yours! You let this rabid beast run around loose?"

Sam's brows came together. "He's not rabid! He's just a puppy. He doesn't always think before he acts. We're working on it, but he's not fully trained yet."

"Like father, like son," she bit out, her gaze going from Sam's tight face to the canine's adoring one.

"As I said, he doesn't know any better," Sam said slowly and distinctly. "You, on the other hand, should know better than to let house cats outside. Belle always kept them inside. That's why she had the sun-room built."

"It's my yard and they need the exercise. They're all overweight. I wanted them to get out for a while. Of course I didn't expect them to be chased by your miserable excuse for a dog." She poked his bare chest. Her finger seemed to sizzle where she touched him and she jumped. Her nail slid across his sweaty pectoral muscle, leaving a long, red scratch.

"Ow!" Sam leapt back and tucked his chin in to look down at the wound she had left.

Dismayed, Laura saw what she'd done. Why was she so clumsy around him? "Oh... Oh, I'm sorry. Do you want me to get some—?"

"I don't want you to do anything," he said, lifting his hands to ward her off. "Except to keep these cats inside."

Insulted, Laura wrapped her own hands protectively around Guinevere. "You seem to have things a little bit backward here. Your dog has no right to be on this property."

Sam pointedly rubbed the scratch she had made. "He has every right to sleep under that hedge, which is the shared property boundary."

Her chin shot up. "Fine. Let him sleep there. But he'd better not chase my cats again or I'll call the animal-control officer."

A satisfied expression came over Sam's face. "It won't do you any good. They'll just bring him back to me."

"What do you mean?"

"I mean there's no dog pound in this town. The town council pays me to board all the strays and find homes for them if I possibly can."

She had been building up a healthy head of steam to blast him with, but he'd taken all the heat out of it. She blinked. "Why you?"

"Because I own Calhoun Kennels. Every stray dog in town is in my backyard."

"The heck you say!" Laura turned and stalked toward the hedge. Standing on tiptoe, she could barely see over the top. Sure enough, the flashes of silver she had seen and assumed was chain-link fencing was a kennel. The yard held a big dog-run and attached roomy pens. At the sight of her, the animals barked in alarm.

That explained the dogs she'd heard lately. Strange that she hadn't figured it out before. But then, she'd been distracted by all that had been going on. She couldn't imagine why Belle had never mentioned Sam's kennels.

Laura dropped back on her heels and swiveled around to confront Sam. "Calhoun Kennels, huh?"

Sam's firm chin bobbed as he nodded. "Dogs bought, sold and boarded. We train sight hunters, bird dogs and gundogs," he said proudly as if he was quoting from an ad in the Yellow Pages.

The wind kicked up and tossed her strawberry-blond curls around her face. She shoved them back impatiently with one hand, clasping Guinevere to her hip with the other. "Well, how come all the rest are penned up and this juvenile delinquent is running loose?"

"I haven't had him very long and I've just started his training." Sam reached down to pat the animal with obvious affection. The pup happily angled his head to slobber on his hand. "Brandy here is a Chesapeake Bay retriever, a bit obstinate and hard to train—"

"No kidding."

"—but worth the effort because they're good hunters and excellent with children," Sam went on as if she hadn't interrupted.

"It's only cats they hate?" she asked sweetly.

Sam grunted impatiently as he stood. "Don't be an idiot. He doesn't hate them. He was just having fun."

Laura lifted Guinevere toward him. "*She* didn't think it was much fun."

She glanced over to see that the other cats were beginning to venture down cautiously. Turning, she marched to the steps leading to the back door and swung it open so that her four-legged charges could hurry in. She dropped Guinevere gently inside and closed the door.

"If you're going to let them out, you'll have to put up a fence." His brows lifted mockingly. "Need some money?"

"I don't see why I should have to fence in my yard to keep out *your* dog," she said through pinched lips.

His narrow, clever face lit with challenge. "It's all part of taking good care of the cats.

If you don't give them the best care possible, you'll lose the inheritance.''

She almost choked on her rage. Her golden-brown eyes narrowed. "That thought seems to make you very happy, but for your information, I *intend* to take good care of them.''

His gaze searched her face, then honed in on the defiance in her eyes. "You're staying, then?''

Laura came down the steps and advanced toward him until she was only inches away. Their noses almost touched. She could smell healthy male sweat, a clean, citrusy scent, and Brandy on him. "You couldn't get me out of here with dynamite, mister.''

"I don't think it'll come to that, Laura. You won't be able to do without your high-flying life-style. You'll need the big city, the big department stores, and go running back to Washington.''

"I've said it before. You know nothing about me or what I can or can't do without.'' She paused, fearing she really would lose her temper. Somehow, her voice stayed level. "I came over this morning to make peace with 'you. I thought that if we're going to be neighbors—if you're going to be involved in settling my great-aunt's estate—we need to get along. I was wrong, of course, because you don't want to get along. You just want to judge me on things you know nothing about."

"If you want to eat regularly, we need to get along." His look was pure innocence. "Unless you intend to exist on that diet of pond scum you suggested yesterday."

Her eyes widened and angry sparks seemed to shower in them. "You wouldn't dare keep that trust account from me just because I think you're an overbearing, insensitive clod."

"Tut, tut, tut." His tongue clicked as he straightened away and surveyed the fury in her face. "You're getting really close to losing control, you know."

Her answer was low and scathing. "Oh, I can get a lot closer, so you'd better watch out. I may have to depend on you for my expense money, a fact that I find galling, but I don't have to like you—and I won't! In a couple of days I'm going to go to Washington, give up my apartment and move my things here. When I need money, you can deposit it in my account at the bank. We'll never have to see each other." She pivoted as gracefully as a ballet dancer and returned to the steps to the back door. Her head was high, as was her color, but she managed to keep calm—barely—though she couldn't help blasting him with one parting shot. "Just stay out of my way and keep that mutt away from my cats."

Sam told the pup to sit and he followed Laura to the stairs, his long legs taking the creaky wooden steps two at a time. "So, the battle lines are drawn, are they? Well, remember, for the next year these had better be the best-kept cats in South Carolina or you'll lose everything."

Because she couldn't think of any answer that didn't involve a number of unladylike four-letter words, Laura turned her back on him and went into the house. She would have liked to slam the door, releasing some of the fury and hatred within her, but she closed it quietly instead. That, more than anything, showed she wasn't going to let him get to her.

Inside, she stomped toward the stairs. At least she understood why the cats hadn't been left to Sam. If the rest of his dogs were anything like Brandy, Belle's poor pets wouldn't have lasted past lunchtime!

CHAPTER FIVE

A FEW MINUTES LATER, Laura was upstairs smoothing the covers on her bed when she was nearly blasted off her feet by a wailing lament about an eighteen-wheel trucker who had lost his only love. She dashed to the window and looked out to see her nemesis, Sam Calhoun, sawing and singing in time to the raucous country music booming from a portable radio sitting on the stump of the apple tree.

She slammed the window shut and sank down on the sill. Not only did she have to put up with him living next door, she had to listen to his music, too. It wasn't fair. She glanced around and her face lit with mischief. She didn't have to listen if she didn't want to.

Pushing away from the window, she crossed the room and began rummaging in the closet. She finally found an old tape player and a set of scratchy, poor-quality Verdi tapes that should have been discarded during her last visit. She had picked them up at a yard sale during her lean college years and quickly discovered they weren't worth even the little she'd paid for them.

Back across the room, she opened the window. Smugly she plugged in the player, popped in the tape of *Rigoletto,* and punched "play." The sound of the orchestra, scratchy and wavering, filled the morning's fresh breeze. Two could play this game. She was going to fight fire with fire. Or, in this case, fight Waylon with Giuseppe!

With a satisfied nod, she finished making the bed, raised the tape player's volume to full blast, and went downstairs to clean the litter boxes.

She spent the rest of the day making plans for the next year. In one of the overflowing kitchen drawers she found a thick legal-size pad and started making a list of all that needed to be done. As she saw it, she had no choice but to sell the house. There was no reason to stay in Webster now that Belle was gone.

She knew that at the end of the year, she'd need to find a place within commuting distance of her job in Washington—when she found another job. A pang of regret twisted inside her, but she fought it down. There would be other jobs, other opportunities.

But it no longer seemed to matter. Sadness and regret weighted her heart. She had the uncomfortable feeling that Sam's accusations about her neglecting Belle were true. If she had tried harder, arranged things better, she might have been able to get home to Belle. Now it was too late.

Laura sat staring at the pad with tear-filled eyes, then resolutely pulled her mind back to the task at hand. The first thing to do was clear out the house and fix it up for sale. She leaned back on the sturdy oak chair and looked around the kitchen. Obviously someone had made a start here. Several cabinet doors had been stripped of paint. She supposed she would have to ask Sam who'd been doing the work for Belle.

There were a great many things she would keep, perhaps even some things her mother would want. She knew she couldn't bear to part with the antiques, some of which had belonged to her own grandparents. Belle had brought them along to make Laura's father feel more at home when he had moved in with her after his parents were killed in a train accident.

There was also a great deal of plain old junk that had to be dealt with. Laura knew the attic was full, as was Belle's bedroom, which she had been avoiding.

Between sorting things, fixing up the house and taking care of the cats, the next year would be busy. She wouldn't have to see Sam Calhoun at all. Irritated that her thoughts had slipped back to him, she picked up her pen and began writing industriously on her tablet. He'd said she had to take good care of the cats. The best way to do that was to take them to the vet and make sure they'd all been spayed or neutered. Belle's will said she had to care for them until they died. Well, fine, but she didn't have to care for their children and grandchildren!

All her ambitious plans were easier to make than to implement. She decided to start sorting at the top of the house and work her way down. With that in mind, she marched up to the attic.

One of the first things she found there was the Blue Onion-patterned tea set she had played with as a child. She sat with one of the delicate china cups cradled in her palm, examining the design. Nostalgia overwhelmed her as she recalled the parties she and Belle had held with the cats as their unwilling guests up in the turret room. Tears pinched her nose and burned her eyes as she relived the conversations they used to have, covering every topic of vital interest to a little girl.

With a soft cry, Laura pushed the cup back into the box and scrambled to her feet. She couldn't do this quite yet. The sorting would have to wait until she came back from Washington. She hurried from the attic and sought solace with the cats in the peaceful sun-room.

A storm rolled in that night, boiling through the skies over the Piedmont area, dropping much-needed rain on tobacco and cotton fields. In Webster, lightning crackled and thunder boomed. Laura spent a restless night, bothered by the heat and humidity and a growing pressure behind her eyes. She woke, groggy and bleary-eyed, to more thunder.

Restlessly she turned over to look at the ceiling, then closed her eyes on a wave of pain as the thunder began again. Her brow furrowed. Since when did thunder have such a regular rhythm? It sounded almost like... hammering!

She sat up so suddenly that pain stabbed through her head. With a heartfelt groan, she slumped on the side of the bed and pressed her palms to her temples until it eased. Pulling on her robe, she listed toward the bedroom door and stumbled down the stairs.

Halfway down, she recognized the cheerful, off-key singing as Sam Calhoun's. The song was the one he'd been listening to the day before, but it sounded even worse coming from him. He was standing in the living room amid yards of drop cloths. Pictures had been removed from the walls and stacked on the sagging sofa. He was on his hands and knees, pounding down a loose baseboard.

Laura viewed it all, then sank onto the bottom step with a moan and closed her eyes. For the second morning in a row Sam had catapulted her out of a sound sleep.

"Do you have a death wish, Calhoun?" she asked him. He didn't answer, so she raised her voice and repeated it. The effort of speaking over the racket he was creating made her head pound even more. Agonized, she clasped her temples between her hands.

Sam turned with a cocky grin to rest on one knee, his forearm propped on it and his hammer dangling from his fingers. "Not particularly." His impudent gaze scanned her rumpled self. "Didn't wake up too cheerful, huh?"

Her elbows rested on her knees as she gently cradled her aching head in a picture of abject misery, and spoke into her lap. "Don't you ever sleep? You always seem to be up at the crack of dawn—or before—making some gosh-awful racket." She opened one eye and glared at him balefully. "I realize you don't have a real job, but don't you have a life? And what are you doing in *my* house?"

Sam sauntered toward her as he slipped the hammer into a loop of the tool belt at his waist.

He was dressed in a pair of cutoffs and an old white T-shirt with "Harvard" printed on it in faded letters. "Some of us don't sleep until nearly noon," he said, thrusting his chin toward the Seth Thomas mantel clock. It was barely nine, Laura noted, but before she could protest he went on, "And I'm in your house because I had an agreement with Belle to do some repairs."

She cast her eyes heavenward in disgust. "I should have guessed," she grumbled, then added. "I suppose you're the one responsible for the mess in the kitchen."

His grin reappeared with its crooked slant. "Hey, it's going to look great. I'll finish in there as soon as the hardware store gets the shade of stain Belle wanted. In the meantime, there's plenty to do in the living room. I built the sun-room and painted the outside of the house," he added.

She sighed. "Why you?"

"Because I have the skills."

"Not to mention the tools," she muttered, eyeing the various objects hanging from his belt. When she realized her gaze was straying to his tight, faded shorts, then following the raveled strings down his hair-dusted thighs, she started in alarm, her face flushing. "I don't want you here," she said firmly. "If there's any fixing up, I'll do it myself or hire someone."

"Oh?" His forehead wrinkled consideringly and his grey eyes came alight with interest. "What do you plan to use for money? I couldn't possibly authorize anything like that since I'm capable of doing the repairs myself. Besides, I promised."

His voice was matter-of-fact, his face bland. Laura wanted to strangle him. Instead she wrapped her hand around the pineapple-shaped newel post to pull herself up. "Listen, Calhoun, we'd better get a few things straight—" She was interrupted by the telephone. Giving him a look that said the discussion wasn't finished, she sank down again and reached through the banister to the phone table beside the stairs.

Sam smirked and began yanking out nails that had held pictures on the walls.

When she lifted the receiver to her ear, a faint, crackling sound coming over the wire told her the call was long distance. "Hello?"

"Laura? Is that you?" Jason Creed's voice sounded faint.

Pleased to hear from him, Laura gripped the receiver closer to her ear and shouted into it, "Yes, Jason, it's me. How are you?"

"What are you doing in South Carolina? Tracking you down is going to cost the earth."

Although the effort of speaking loudly made her head hurt even more, Laura started to tell him about Belle's death, but he cut her off.

"Yes, your mother told me all about it when she gave me this number, but the funeral's over, isn't it? I thought you'd be heading back to Washington."

Miffed that he didn't offer condolences on Belle's death, Laura told herself that he'd probably been worried when he couldn't locate her. Worry always made him short-tempered. "I can't yet. I've got to clear things up here."

Across the room, Sam sent her a faintly disapproving glance as he bent to open a can of filler to patch the nail holes. She watched the way his T-shirt stretched over the banded muscles of his back and separated from the waist of his shorts. Shivers racked her as she drew her attention back to what Jason was saying.

"How long will it take? They won't hold that job for you very long. I used my connections to get that job for you, but I won't be responsible if you blow it."

His connections? She held the receiver away and stared at it. She must be hearing things. He had vaguely mentioned in passing that someone he knew was looking for an executive assistant. Laura had pursued, and landed, the position on her own.

She wrinkled her nose in consternation, re-calling that for all his good points, Jason could be somewhat pompous. If anything permanent was to develop between them, he'd have to change that unfortunate trait. She wasn't going to get into a discussion about it now, though, while Sam Calhoun was in the same room.

Uncomfortably she glanced at him. Sam was cheerfully slapping on filler and smoothing it. His diligence didn't fool her for a second. He was listening to everything she said. She turned her back to him. She would have to be careful about what she said to Jason.

"I won't be taking the job, after all, Jason."

"What?" he squawked. "You can't be serious."

Exasperated, Laura took a deep breath and, with Sam as an avid audience, told Jason about the terms of Belle's will, about having to live in the house for a year before she could sell it.

"Well, then, of course, you must stay," he said in a smooth voice, hastily back-pedaling. "This is quite an opportunity for, uh, you. You could do a great deal with that kind of money."

Her gaze flew automatically to Sam who had stopped all pretense of work and was listening unabashedly. He was tapping a putty knife against his palm and watching her with narrowed eyes. A chill swept over her. What was he thinking? The worst, no doubt. "Yes, of course, but the money isn't—"

"Yours yet?" Jason broke in. "Too bad, but you'll see, this year will go faster than you think, and then you can use it for whatever you want."

Laura's heart plummeted to the region of her navel. This was getting out of hand. Jason's tone was the same calm, understanding one he always used, but there was an underlying note that bothered her. However she couldn't pursue that now, and explain about using the inheritance for her brother and sister's education, not with Sam listening. "I'll think about that later," she said quietly.

They talked a few more minutes and Laura mentally ticked off the reasons she liked Jason. He was smart and ambitious and they had a great deal in common, including their mutual love for art and music. She admitted that he talked about money too much, but she put that down to his being raised by his single mother, who had worked at menial jobs all her life. Jason had literally pulled himself up by his bootstraps and made himself into the urbane kind of man he wanted to be.

She recalled the time, three years ago, when Belle had met Jason in Paris and said she could tell he was ambitious. Laura had been vaguely disturbed by this faint praise, but was sure Belle would like him once she got to know him.

"Well, I should go," he finally said. "Transatlantic calls cost a fortune, you know. You just stay right there and take care of your aunt's cats and her estate. Don't let this opportunity slip away."

"I won't, Jason," she answered automatically, but for some reason her traitorous eyes slid to Sam's obviously interested face. She hung up and prepared herself for the questions she knew were coming—although she certainly didn't owe him any answers! Another chill shook her. Disturbed, she ran a hand through her tousled curls.

"Somebody special?"

She avoided his eyes. "Yes, Jason Creed...a good friend."

"Sounds like more than a friend. Are you going to marry him? I'll bet he's just as interested in Belle's money as you are."

Fire snapped into her eyes. "Now you listen here, Calhoun. You have no right to judge me." Laura grabbed the newel post and tugged herself upwards. The world tilted crazily, then went dark as she toppled in a dead faint.

LAURA AWOKE WITH A START to the pungent bite of ammonia. She turned her head away, gagged and coughed, then opened her eyes to find that Sam had carried her upstairs. He hovered anxiously above her, holding a big bottle of household cleaner under her nose, waving it back and forth frantically.

She wondered with a trace of hysteria if he was trying to kill her or just burn up her sinuses. "That's enough," she choked, lifting a hand to ward him off. Tears formed in reaction to the chemical and spurted into her eyes. "I'm awake."

Sam moved aside, still holding the noxious liquid, and watched her with a furious look. "You scared the hell out of me. How come women don't carry smelling salts like they did a hundred years ago?" he asked irrationally. "I had to run downstairs for this stuff." He waved the bottle, releasing another cloud of pungent aroma.

"Sam," Laura gasped, "put that away before you kill me."

He capped it hastily, muttering. "Damned clever to think of it, even if I do say so myself."

He looked so aggrieved, Laura couldn't help offering a shaky smile. "Brilliant."

Sam's eyes narrowed and his thick brows drew together over his prominent nose. "What's the matter with you? You're burning up with fever."

Laura closed her eyes as she lifted trembling hands and attempted to pull her robe more tightly around her. It was caught beneath her hips and ridged under her back. Her short cotton nightgown had ridden up her thighs. A lot more of her was exposed than she would have liked, but it required too much effort to lift herself up and rearrange everything. And she certainly couldn't ask Sam to do it for her. The thought of his hands on her sent another flush of fever though her, and goose bumps rose on her arms. She cast him a defensive look, then closed her eyes again and sighed. "You have a lousy bedside manner."

"Yeah, well, it doesn't get much exercise." He perched on the side of the bed, his long, muscled thigh against her hip, and looked down at her. "Open your eyes. I want to check your pupils."

"I don't have a concussion. Just a fever."

"Open them, anyway."

She knew he'd pry them open and probably prop them with toothpicks if she didn't obey, so Laura let her eyelids flutter up. He was bending over her. Anxiety lined his roughly hewn face.

He gazed into her eyes for a moment, then touched the tip of her nose. She lifted a weak hand to bat him away. "It's a dog's nose you check for fever. In humans, you feel their cheeks."

"I know that. I'm a kennel owner, re-member?" he answered gruffly, his thick lashes sweeping down to hide his expression. "How long have you been feeling bad?"

"Just since last night."

"Do you think it's the flu?"

"No. It feels like malaria."

He straightened. "Malaria! You're kid-ding!"

"No, I'm not. Almost everyone in Senegal gets it."

"Living in the embassy compound?" Skep-ticism was ripe in his voice and face.

Laura was too drained to argue with him. She turned on her side, away from him, and said, "I didn't live in the embassy compound. I was just a secretary with a small apartment in Dakar. Besides, malaria is spread by mos-quitoes, which are everywhere. And I spent weeks out in the country—"

"Doing what?" he prompted from behind her when she broke off. He stroked her shoulder gently.

Laura burrowed her head into the pillow, too tired to fight him. His hand felt so good. She wanted to arch against it like a spoiled cat. There was a reason she shouldn't tell him very much about herself, but right now she couldn't remember what it was. "I was helping the Red Cross pass out food staples in the villages. Because of the drought, the Senegalese hadn't had a good millet or peanut crop..." Her voice died away tiredly.

His hand stilled, tightened, then fell away. "I'm going to take you to the doctor."

"No," she protested groggily. "I just need some medicine. Quinine."

"You're going to the doctor. Can you dress yourself, or do you want me to do it?"

Her eyes flew open and she rolled over to bump against his bare knee. "Don't even try it!"

A grin glimmered on his lips. "Then get up and do it yourself while I call the doctor's office and tell them I'm bringing you in."

He stood and strode to the door without looking back. If she'd had the strength, she would have thrown something at him. As it was, she rested for a moment, then, shivering, got up and put on the shorts and shirt she had worn the day before and slipped her feet into her sandals. She staggered to the bathroom to wash her face and drag a comb through her sweat-tangled curls. She was sitting on the side of the bed, trembling with chills and fever, when Sam bounded into the room.

"It's all set. Dr. Clay can work you in right away."

She lifted a weary face toward him, unsure whether she hated him more for his energy or his high-handedness. "If you'll just ask him to prescribe some medicine, I'm sure he'd do it," she explained patiently. "Malaria isn't exactly unheard of in South Carolina, you know."

"Well, *I've* never had it," he said in a disgustingly robust voice. "Besides, I don't want you complaining that I didn't take good care of you while you were sick."

"I don't want you taking care of me at *all* while I'm sick!"

He ignored her, approaching the bed and scooping her up once again. "Belle would expect it of me," he said implacably as he settled her against his chest.

She would have fought him, held herself stiffly erect, objected vehemently, Laura assured herself, if only she had more strength.

What she finally did was slump on him and thank her lucky stars he had a T-shirt covering his chest. If she'd come into direct contact with his warm, vital skin. Dr. Clay would surely have ordered a hospital stay while she recovered from the effects.

In a remarkably short time he had her downstairs, out the door and into the cab of his crummy old truck, freshly dented thanks to her. She winced at the memory and wilted against the frayed upholstery.

Sam saw the look as he slammed her door. When he got in, he turned on the engine, which sounded worse than ever, and hooked a gentle hand behind her neck. "Why don't you put your head down here," he said, tapping his other palm against his thigh.

Her eyes widened in horror. He had to be kidding! "No, I'll be all right."

Maybe he decided it was a bad idea, too. Instead he pulled her beside him and cradled her head on his shoulder. Telling herself she'd protest his take-charge attitude just as soon as she felt better, she sank gratefully against him.

"Sorry I have to take you in this old thing, but the Thunderbird won't be ready for another week," he said quietly, his gaze on her flushed face. He sounded truly regretful and not the least bit upset that she was the cause of his car problems.

"That's all right," she murmured, letting her head rest on his shoulder and her eyelids settle shut.

They started off, his shifting and driving so smooth she could have balanced a full teacup on her lap. She felt ridiculously secure with him, considering there was no love lost between them.

At Dr. Clay's office, he whisked her inside and even accompanied her into the examining room. As if she was a two-year-old with an ear infection, she thought, disgruntled. But it was his arm she held as she shuffled down the hall, his hands she allowed to clasp her waist and boost her onto the high examining table. He made her lie down with her head on a paper-covered pillow, then sat on a chair beside her.

After a few minutes, the doctor bustled in. He was small and energetic with a full head of white hair and a grandfatherly air that he had probably perfected straight out of medical school forty years before. He confirmed Laura's self-diagnosis and said the attack was probably brought on by the changes in climate and barometric pressure from Africa, to Alaska, to Washington, then to Webster. He had her and Sam out the door, prescription in hand, in twenty minutes.

Such efficiency in the usually sleepy little town made Laura feel almost breathless. Just as efficiently, Sam picked up the medicine at the drugstore and took her back home. Though she'd only been out of bed briefly, she felt drained by her exertions and followed in a feverish stupor as Sam gave her the medicine and tucked her, still-clothed, into bed.

Within minutes she was drifting into sleep. She felt something brush her brow and caught a whiff of a familiar, citrusy scent. For a moment she felt an odd warmth, not unlike the fever, that she wanted to consider and savor. She tried to fight the darkness, but it claimed her.

That day and the next were a haze of waking and sleeping. Sam always seemed to be there, supporting her head for drinks of water, juice or broth. She hated the last, almost spewing it on him when he got it close enough for her to discover that it wasn't apple juice.

He sat behind her, propped her against his chest, which felt as hard as the door of a bank vault, and held her head in a firm but gentle grip. "This will give you strength," he claimed, bringing the cup to her lips.

"I only want enough strength to pour this broth over your head," she muttered against the rim.

His voice was low and sexy in his throat. "Tut, tut, tut, Laura. You've really got to try to overcome this tendency to go all fluttery and weepy with gratitude."

Before she could think of a clever reply, he had settled her back on the pillows with careful hands and she had drifted off again.

On the second afternoon, her fever broke and she woke up clear-eyed but weak as a kitten and sore all over. She gazed out the window at the lengthening shadows. If she had to suffer through a bout of malaria every time the weather changed, this was going to be a miserable year.

CHAPTER SIX

"OH, YOU'RE AWAKE." Sam made the triumphant observation as he entered the room with yet another glass of some concoction he expected her to drink. He rounded the bed and sat beside her in a way that was becoming all too familiar. The worn knee of his jeans was only inches from her thigh.

Laura edged away as she eyed the glass. It was frothing with a mixture that looked as if it had just gone through the blender. "What is it this time?" she asked warily as she pushed herself into a sitting position. She was careful to keep the sheet and light blanket pulled up over her flimsy cotton nightgown. Sam Calhoun had seen a good deal more of her in the past few days than she'd ever intended.

His quick, intelligent eyes seemed to gauge the alertness in her expression, and his crooked smile appeared. "Welcome back to the land of the living." He waved the glass invitingly. "It's bananas, plain yogurt and pears, with a few other secret ingredients. I thought you might need some protein and vitamins.''

Although she winced at the sound of it, she accepted the glass and took a healthy swallow. Consideringly, she let it wash over her tongue. "Why, it's delicious!"

"Old family recipe," he answered with pride. "I used to make it for my mom whenever she had another baby. It's great for nursing mothers."

Laura choked and coughed. "I'm not a nursing mother!"

His gaze drifted to where her front was safely hidden beneath the covers. "No, but you need strength. It all works on the same principle."

Tingling sensations shivered through her. Dismayed, Laura latched onto what he had said earlier. "*Another* baby?"

He nodded. "I'm the oldest of five. Three boys and two girls."

In these days of two-child families, it was unusual to meet someone with a family as large as hers. She smiled. "I'm the oldest of six."

"I know. Belle showed me all their pictures."

Laura looked up at him, her golden-brown eyes taking in his warm, inviting smile. Her tongue touched the corner of her mouth. "I didn't know that about you, although she mentioned you in her letters a lot." Belle hadn't

told her the important things, though. She had
said he was helpful and considerate, but she'd
never described his physical appearance. She'd
never told Laura about the way his sable-brown
hair curled down over his collar or the way his
gray eyes missed nothing. She hadn't described
the sinewy strength of his body or the way he
could carry a 130 pound woman up a flight of
stairs. . . .

Thinking of all he'd done for her in the past
two days, Laura felt a stream of pleasure well
up and spread through her. For some reason,
she couldn't remember why she needed to keep
her distance from him.

She lifted the glass and drank, then licked
the frothy mustache from her top lip. She froze
when she saw that Sam was watching the tip
of her tongue darting in and out. Slowly she
lowered the glass to her lap.

"What did Belle tell you about me?" Sam
tilted his head and leaned forward as if he expected her to whisper her answer and he didn't
want to miss what she had to say. His thick
lashes concealed his expression, and Laura
found that it made him seem vulnerable, yet
masculine in a way she had never noticed with
any other man.

Her fingers tightened on the frosty glass. The
palm of that hand was suddenly the only cool

thing about her. Her fever seemed to be returning in a wave. "That you were . . . hurt and mad at the world. That you were working on the house next door. That the two of you enjoyed philosophical discussions. She liked you a great deal." Her eyes were wide and honest. "Admired you."

With a slow, easy movement that could have gentled a skittish pony, Sam reached out and took the glass from her, then set it on the nightstand. All the time, his gaze held hers. "And what do you think? Now that you've had a chance to get to know me. Do you think I took advantage of her? Do you think I coerced her into making me her executor?"

She caught her lip between her teeth. "I . . ."

"Because I didn't," he continued inexorably. "I didn't. In New York, I had a small brokerage house. When things went sour on the market and in my life, I lost a lot. I moved here and got to know your great-aunt. She taught me how little value there really is in money." His crooked smile glimmered. "But she was willing to let me advise her on investments. That's why she felt she could trust me." His head tilted lazily, but his eyes never left her face. "Do you think she was wrong to trust me?"

At the sincere intensity in his face, the hint of sorrow, Laura drew a quick breath. She felt as if something familiar was trying to force its way into her senses. But she couldn't take the time to decide what it was, because she was considering Sam's question. Her own face was earnest as she answered, "I think Belle did exactly what she wanted to do, just as she always had in life."

Sam's hand reached for hers and he threaded his calloused fingers between her trembling ones. "We've gone about this all wrong, you know. We've both lost someone we loved. We should be comforting each other."

"Comforting?" The word squeezed out of her constricted lungs. Laura didn't understand what was happening. She had never experienced this strange, restless itch before. It must be some new aftereffect of the malaria. She wanted to lean into him, to crawl right into his lap and pull his solid arms around her.

Mesmerized, she watched Sam's face come closer, the pupils of his eyes dilating with pleasure even as his lids half closed. He looked down at her lips, then up to meet her eyes, touching each point of her face, from the freckles that lay in careless sprinkles across her nose to the high thrust of her cheekbones, then back to her trembling mouth.

He reached over to cup her jaw. The river of pleasure that had sprung free rushed into her heart, increasing its beat. And yet, the sense of familiarity plagued her, teasing at her memory until she seemed to be smelling...

"Cashmere Bouquet!" she blurted.

"What?" Sam blinked and pulled his head away.

The scent filled her nose. Forgetting about the sheet so carefully tucked under her arms, she sat upright and glanced around. She lifted her hands as if to gather in the fragrance that was already dissipating. "The bath powder. Don't you smell it?"

The moment—whatever it had been—was shattered. Sam sat back and looked around, blinking as if he had just staggered out of a dark tunnel. "I don't smell anything."

Laura came slowly to her knees and gazed around. The room looked the same. The blue-flowered curtains moved gently in the balmy breeze drifting in the window. Her suitcase was open on the chair, her light cotton robe spilling out of it. "You must smell it. It's the one—"

She snapped her mouth shut, realizing it would sound silly if she said it was the powder Belle had always used. Sitting back abruptly on her heels, she gathered up the fallen sheet and held it to her chin. What was the matter with her? For a moment she had felt as if there were forces at work in the room that she didn't understand. Her fingers fluttered helplessly and she slumped against the pillows, plucking at the covers. Her lashes swept down and she glanced at Sam's puzzled face from beneath them. "Oh, nothing. I guess I'm imagining things."

He frowned, then shrugged as he picked up the glass. "Here. Finish this." When his hands neared her face, she realized that was where the scent was coming from. He must have washed his hands with the bar of Cashmere Bouquet soap by the kitchen sink.

Feeling silly at her overreaction, she obediently drank the yogurt mixture as she considered the strange moment that had just passed. She was certain that she would have kissed Sam if he had leaned the tiniest bit closer. Thank goodness her overactive imagination had kept her from doing something extremely foolish.

She wasn't going to get involved with Sam Calhoun. She'd had too many upheavals in her life in the past week. She felt shaky and confused and unsure of what was happening to her. The career she had loved and worked hard to establish had been temporarily tossed out the window. She had just lost her beloved aunt.

No, she definitely wasn't going to get involved with him.

Satisfied with that decision, she finished the yogurt drink and handed the glass back to Sam, giving him a semblance of a cheery smile. "That was delicious. Thank you."

He took the empty glass and stood up. Laura told herself it was relief and not disappointment that she felt when he moved across the room.

"Do you feel like getting up and coming downstairs? Maybe outside?"

"Outside?" She whispered the word with all the reverence of someone being offered a glimpse of paradise. She hated being cooped up.

He grinned and lifted his chin, laughing silently at her. "I'm working with some puppies. Thought you might like to watch."

"Oh? What are you doing with them?"

"Get out of that bed, come over to my place and find out." He put his hand on the doorjamb, then looked back. "Unless you need me to help you get dressed?" he asked with a parody of a leer.

"Hit the road, Calhoun," she ordered, pointing her thumb toward the stairs.

He shrugged then sauntered away. "I'll be at the kennel."

Eagerly, Laura swung her feet out of bed and stood. To her relief, she experienced no lightness or aching in her head, although she felt a little weak and decidedly in need of a shower. She grimaced at the clothes piled in her suitcase. The few things she had packed were either dirty or inappropriate. In the closet she found a sundress she had worn in college. It was a faded blue print, but perfectly wearable. She hesitated, running her fingers over the soft cotton, until she firmly reminded herself that she wasn't trying to impress Sam Calhoun.

Once she was showered and dressed, she went downstairs, glad to be free of her enforced confinement. The living room was still a shambles, with no apparent progress made on the painting he had started the previous morning. Laura examined it all with a frown, remembered the unfinished kitchen cabinets and wondered if he was the type of person who never finished what he started. Jolted, she realized she'd been thinking about the kiss that had almost occurred upstairs. Thrusting the thought aside, she walked resolutely through the house to check on the cats.

The seven felines seemed glad to see her, twining around her legs and almost tripping her. She spent a few minutes with them, noted that they had clean litter and fresh water, then went over to Sam's.

She followed a brick path around the side of his house, admiring the carefully tended rosebushes in their pristine beds. At the gate she pulled the latch release, and it swung open to admit her to his domain.

Laura kept her hand on the open gate as she glanced around. The yard she remembered as a weed-choked jungle was almost austere in its neatness. The kennel and dog run were shaded by beech and maple trees, and the grass has closely mowed.

In the roomy pens she counted six dogs, including the ungovernable Brandy, who barked a greeting that was quickly echoed by his pals.

Sam was sitting in the center of the yard, his long legs forming a V in front of him. He turned when he heard her. "Shut the gate. I don't want these guys to get out."

She hurried to do as he said, at the same time looking back over her shoulder to see who the "guys" were. Delighted, she spied six puppies clustered about his knees. One of them broke from the pack and started waddling toward her on his fat little legs. She stopped as he sniffed her sandaled feet, then watched in amazement as he stiffened and quivered, his head down and his tiny tail jutting straight out.

"Did you go in to see the cats before you came over?" Sam asked.

"Why, yes."

"He smells them." Sam's voice held the pride of a new father. "Come over here and he'll follow."

Laura laughed as she stepped gingerly around the inquisitive little fellow. Sure enough, he followed the intriguing new scent. "Between the cats and the pups, I won't be able to call my ankles my own."

Sam's gaze flicked to her shapely legs. "Believe me, Laura, nobody could mistake those for anyone else's. Here. Sit down and watch." He got up and found a small stool for her, then resumed his seat on the grass.

Tucking her skirt behind her knees, she positioned herself carefully on the too-short stool. Her knees were bent under her chin, but she wasn't uncomfortable. Like Sam, she let her hands dangle. The puppies tumbled over each other to explore the interesting guest, but the one who had greeted her acted as if she was his personal property. He nudged the others aside to test his small teeth against her fingers.

She scooped him into her lap and ran her hands over the brown spots on his ears and head, kneading his white back. "What kind are they?"

"Pointers." He nodded toward the one in her lap. "That one's going to make the best gundog of the litter."

Her hand paused and her face lit with curiosity. "How do you know?"

"Breeding, for one thing. Rounder and Misty over there are their parents." Sam gestured to the kennel where a pair of pointers could be seen stretched out, asleep.

Laura grinned. They were worn out from the rigors of parenthood, no doubt. Her mom and Harry had looked something like that for weeks after each of her siblings had been born.

"He's got some of the best pointer's blood in the world in him," Sam continued. "Both his parents have soft mouths—that means they don't maul game they've picked up for the hunter."

"Oh, I see," she said, humoring him in his enthusiasm, but not really seeing at all.

"Training, for another," Sam went on, ignoring her amusement. "Look." He took the puppy from her and set him on the ground. From beside him, he picked up a fishing pole with a piece of white cloth attached to it. He dangled it before the curious animal, but instead of making a grab for it, the chubby little guy merely pointed toward it with his nose and went perfectly still.

Laura blinked and laughed in astonishment. "You taught him that?"

"No. It was born in him. The others, too," he said, indicating the rest of the puppies who had by now discovered the cloth. "He's just the best of the litter." Excitement sang in his voice and simmered in his eyes. "I think he'll be the best dog I've trained. I can't wait to take him on field trials."

"What's that?"

Sam launched into a long explanation about how hunting dogs are trained and then entered in competitions. His narrow face took on a glow that made his features even more fascinating. He was passionate about the subject, and Laura found herself becoming interested in it, too.

When he stopped for breath, she asked, "You actually make your living training hunting dogs?"

"That's right."

"Does it pay well?" She couldn't imagine anyone being able to support themselves by training dogs.

His brows lifted in amusement. "When this pup's ready for a new owner, he'll bring me plenty." He mentioned a figure that made Laura's jaw sag.

"For a dog?" she asked weakly.

"Not just any dog," he said, looking truly affronted. "One trained by the best."

"You're certainly sure of yourself."

"Why not?" He raised a shoulder negligently. "I learned from a master—my father."

"Does he still train them, too?"

His gaze touched her and then shifted away. He stared off into the ragged stand of oaks that marked the edge of the stream. "He died when I was fifteen. A hunting accident."

Her hand flew to her mouth. "Oh, Sam. I'm so sorry." She looked down at the puppies, who were now sleeping at their feet. "Then how can you...?"

"Train hunting dogs? Why not? They weren't responsible for his accident."

Her eyes filled with consternation and concern. "I'm sorry. I didn't mean to pry."

"I brought it up, Laura," he reminded her, but then he was silent for a minute, his hand running smoothly down the back of one of the pups. "We lived where hunting was very popular and his dogs were considered the best. He taught me everything he'd learned over the years, but after he died I turned my back on it. I didn't even own a dog until I moved here." Sam's head came up and his arms spread to encompass the yard. "Belle convinced me to give this a try after I'd gutted the house, then practically rebuilt it and got started on the yard." His smile sent a glow of warmth through her. "She used to bring me endless glasses of iced tea—just like you did the other day."

"I'm glad she was here to help you."

"Me, too. I've built something good, something that would have made my father proud." He chuckled. "Hell, it makes *me* proud."

Laura clasped her hands around her knees and arched her back as she lifted her face to stare up at the leaves of a beech tree. "I guess we all look for ways to please our parents, even if we're adults. My father was killed in Vietnam, and I often wonder if he would have approved of the way I turned out."

"Your great-aunt did."

She raised one eyebrow. "But you don't."

Sam's wealth of lashes dropped to hide the expression in his eyes. "I may have overreacted a bit when we first met—"

"You acted like a jerk."

"That, too," he admitted with an unrepentant grin.

Somehow it seemed easier to talk to him sitting in his backyard with a mound of sleeping canines at her feet and with the memory of how he had cared for her during her bout of malaria. They had a great deal in common besides their love for Belle. Surely they could build a friendship on that—once a few problems were cleared up. And as long as she didn't take things too seriously.

She looked down at her lap, then up at him contritely. Color washed her cheeks. "I'm sorry I wrecked your truck and car, and destroyed that poor apple tree," she blurted.

To her surprise, Sam reached over and wrapped one of his long, tough hands around hers. "That's another lesson I've learned in the past few years. It doesn't pay to put your trust in material things. There are more important things. Family, a place of your own, work you can be proud of."

She leaned closer to him, her face a study in wonder. "What made you reach this point, Sam? The problems in New York?"

Regret chased pain across his face. "Yes."

The emotions in him seemed to call out to her and she wanted to reach over to cradle his jaw, but she didn't. Her pulses pounding in alarm, she got to her feet, moving away in a swirl of blue fabric, putting some distance between them. What had she been about to do? Complicate everything, no doubt. "Well, I'm glad you've found work that you really like," she babbled, her eyes darting around the yard, looking at everything but him. "Good luck. Thanks for sharing the puppies with me."

Turning, she hurried out the gate and over to her own house. She dashed up the front steps and shut the door behind her, then stood in the middle of the entryway with her palms pressed to her cheeks. Her reactions to Sam were all skewed. From anger and animosity she had swung to gratitude and now admiration. She actually liked him and was beginning to see what Belle had found so worthy in him. He had integrity and pride in a job well done, but she couldn't start thinking that he...

Laura laughed quickly and breathlessly at her own folly. "Why, he's just my neighbor, and...and the man I have to go to for money." Her voice sounded confident in the still house. "I'm acting as if he'd suggested an illicit affair."

Of course she could be friendly to him, be interested in his life. It was the neighborly thing to do. In a town as small as Webster, it was the *expected* thing to do. She squared her shoulders and headed into the kitchen to feed the cats and fix herself some dinner.

For a moment, she had let her sympathy and understanding overrule her good sense, but that wouldn't happen again. She was sure of it. She was so sure that she said it out loud three more times when she caught herself leaning against the kitchen counter, smiling foolishly and thinking about him.

LAURA HAD a breezy, cheerful expression in place the next morning when Sam arrived. He asked how she was feeling, nodded at her reply, then headed straight into the living room.

He stood with his hands resting loosely on his hips as he examined the room. "I'm going to start painting in here."

She followed him. "Oh, I thought you'd abandoned the project."

He gave her a sharp look. The reserve in her manner must have been obvious to him because he said, "You think that because I raise and train hunting dogs I don't work."

Embarrassment kept her from meeting his gaze. "Don't be silly," she said evasively. "I told you yesterday that I was glad you found something you like to do."

Sam snorted and gave her condescending statement the reply it deserved by ignoring it completely.

"I didn't finish this because you were sick, and I thought the odor might bother you." He knelt beside a can of paint and pulled a small screwdriver from his back pocket. With quick flicks of his wrist, he popped the can open and began stirring the paint with a flat wooden stick. He paused significantly before he said in an even tone, "You seem to be sensitive to smells."

Laura felt the color flood her face as she remembered the scene in her room. She took a deep breath. "Will you be able to finish this today? I'm going to go to Washington tomorrow to get my things and..."

"You don't want me in your house while you're gone?"

She crossed her arms. She didn't know what she'd been trying to say, except that she needed some distance from him. Somehow it seemed too disconcertingly cozy for him to be in the house while she was gone. It would be so easy for her to depend on him, to think of him working here at home while she was off on business. It would seem as though they were a team—or a couple. "I don't mean that, exactly. You'll have to come in and feed the cats."

Sam turned, resting on one knee. "Well, at least I'm good for something in your opinion. If you want this done today, you're going to have to help." He raised his brows as if daring her to argue.

Laura decided it wasn't worth it. Her feelings for him were so puzzling that she couldn't begin to explain her reluctance to have him in her house. She whirled around and hurried up the stairs, wondering when she had begun thinking of the place as hers.

In her room, she changed into a pair of old slacks and a shirt she must have left there during some previous visit. Examining herself in the mirror, she marveled at her selfishness, at the way she had left things behind and expected Belle to watch out for them or save them for her, but it showed how at home she'd always felt here. Something about that thought disturbed her almost as much as her conflicting emotions for Sam. With unsteady hands, she tied her hair up in an old green scarf.

Downstairs again, she accepted a brush and a small container of paint from Sam, who told her to begin with the ornate molding at the top of the walls. Since he was using his own shiny aluminum ladder, she went into the kitchen and got Belle's old wooden stepladder.

Together they pushed the furniture into the center of the room and covered it with thin plastic drop cloths that billowed and puffed at the slightest breeze from the open windows. Since it was early, the heat and humidity hadn't yet grown unbearable, and they began working in companionable silence. Sam rolled the paint over the ceiling in smooth, easy strokes, the stark whiteness looking pristine as it covered the dingy stains on the plaster.

Laura watched him for a moment, her attention caught by his careful, economical movements. When she realized how long she'd been standing entranced by the play of muscles on his back, she started, turned and climbed cautiously to the top step of the creaky wooden ladder, paint can in hand. Frowning, she looked down and swayed experimentally to see if it would hold her. When it only protested slightly at her weight, she went to work, dipping her small brush in and out of the delicate little swirls of the molding.

When Sam finished putting the white paint on the ceiling and began opening cans of covering for the walls, she glanced down, and her eyes darkened in dismay. "Gray?"

He looked up, mouth quirking with amusement. "You don't like it?"

She grimaced. "No. Who picked it out?"

"Your aunt."

Her nose crinkled. "But she loved *bright* colors."

"Maybe she decided it was time for something more conservative."

"That's more than conservative," she said dryly. "It's dull." She leaned heavily on the creaking ladder to continue her argument. "If

I'm going to be living here, I think *I* should be the one to pick out the paint.''

"But you're not going to be living here," he said, his eyes direct, his off-center smile coming into arrogant play. "At least not after this year. You're going to sell the place, remember? And how do you know the new owners won't like this color?''

He was right, of course, although she hated to admit it. She didn't really mind the color of the paint. It would probably be much lighter once it was on the walls, and it might make a nice contrast to the pure white ceiling. She was simply trying to establish some boundaries. Hadn't she decided just last night that all she had to do was be neighborly? She didn't have to let him take over her life. Her hand tightened around the small can. "What colors have you chosen for the other rooms?''

He shrugged, examining his paint roller with exaggerated concern. She thought she detected a gleam in his eye but couldn't be sure. "Same thing.''

"You're kidding! The whole house is going to be the same color?''

Sam dropped his roller into the tray. "Why not? I can get a great deal if I buy the paint in five-gallon buckets.''

Laura slapped her brush into the can so that paint spattered up the insides. "I won't have it."

He surged to his feet and stalked over to her. "You have no choice. It's done, and why should it matter to you?"

"Because I'll be living here!" She should have felt superior, towering over him like this; instead, she felt vulnerable balancing on the rickety ladder.

"Only for a year," he shot back. "You can stand it for that long!"

"I don't even think I'll be able to stand *you* for that long!" She pointed an accusing finger at him. The ladder shifted beneath her feet. Alarmed, she tried to catch herself, scrabbling for a hold on the windowsill, but her nails just scraped along it. She threw her other hand out, splashing paint across the screen and losing her grip on the small can, which dropped onto the sill. Her flailing movements made the ladder shift again. Laura lurched backward and, by some miracle, managed to bump down the two small steps and land on her feet. Her knees buckled from the impact, but Sam was there to grab her around the waist and haul her up against his chest.

The breath was slammed out of her lungs and she tossed her head back as she gasped for air. She noticed the surprised look on Sam's face, then watched as amusement took over.

"When did you get to be so clumsy?" he asked in a low voice, his gray eyes warming dangerously. "You've really got to learn to be more careful."

"I'm ca...hareful," she defended in a wheezy tone. Her paint-flecked hands had somehow come to rest high on his upper arms where his shoulders protruded from the cutoff sleeves of his T-shirt. Beneath her fingertips, his biceps were as hard and rounded as green apples.

"No, you're not. You lose your temper and then you lose control. Belle told me all about you, but she never said you had such a temper."

"I don't. I..." Her protest faded away as she tried to form an argument. Words seemed to float randomly through her mind, but none of them were the ones she knew she should say. Instead, she was thinking how devastatingly attractive his mouth was, especially when he smiled at her. She thought how tall he was, how manly. She thought how right it was to be standing before an open window in a room that reeked of paint, waiting for whatever happened next. Her gaze passed slowly over his face. Something white-hot touched the ends of her nerves then; despite herself, she let her feelings show by the widening of her eyes and the quick intake of her breath.

Sam's hands rested on her hips, then moved just enough to come up under her loose shirt and spread their length and breadth over her skin.

"I've been thinking a lot about kissing you," he admitted, tucking his chin under in a way that pulled his lips down in a sensual slant.

"You have?" Her voice quavered.

"Yes, but I don't think I'll do it."

"Oh?"

"I wouldn't know how to kiss a tall woman."

"Oh?"

"Nah." His pupils dilated, betraying his pleasure, putting the lie to his words. "I wouldn't know what to do if I didn't get a pain in my neck from bending over to kiss a short woman. It adds a certain excitement."

"Well, I don't want to kiss you, either." She raised her head defiantly. It was a mistake because it brought her lips within a whisper of his. She could feel his breath teasing her mouth. "You're . . . you're, ah . . ."

"Exactly." He nodded solemnly, then tilted his head and let his nose trail along the curve of her cheek. He inhaled deeply, raggedly.

"What's so great about two mouths touching, anyway?"

"Nuh...huthing."

"Not a damn thing," he agreed. Humor had long since faded from his eyes. His abundant lashes fell and he muttered something that sounded like, "Oh, damn," before he pressed his mouth against hers.

His lips were firm, tentative at first, then more demanding, asking things of her that she didn't understand. One of his hands came up from her waist to cradle the arch of her throat. Excitement sizzled through her in shocking waves. She had never felt anything as intense as the possession of his lips, the warmth of his hand cradling her head.

Only a very foolish woman would kiss him back, open her lips to his in unmistakable invitation, slide her hands over his shoulders to clasp the back of his neck. And a very foolish woman did all those things—and more.

As she melted against him, Sam took advantage, pulling her closer to his hard body. The only soft thing about him was his mouth, devouring hers.

Such intensity couldn't last, though, without reaching its natural conclusion. Neither of them was ready for that. Sam returned to his senses before she did, breaking away slowly and reluctantly.

She looked up, shocked, at what she'd been doing. Embarrassed, she let her hands flutter down to hang limply at her sides. She breathed in, then out, and swallowed a couple of times as she tried to regain her mental balance. What kind of craziness had overtaken her? She had never reacted this way to a kiss from Jason.

Sam's face was as disturbed as hers, but he recovered more quickly. He started to speak, cleared his throat, then started again. "How do you feel about softball?"

CHAPTER SEVEN

LAURA RESTED HER PALMS on her thighs and leaned forward to watch the action in the batter's box. The setting sun speared its dying rays under the bill of her cap, which had Calhoun Kennels Pointers printed in block letters just about where her brain should have been.

She didn't know how she'd let Sam talk her into substituting on his softball team, but here she was in center field, trying to reaccustom herself to something she hadn't felt since high school—the inside of a fielder's leather glove. Her uniform was made up of spare pieces borrowed from the other members. The shirt was too snug and the pants too loose, but at least they were tailored with a woman's rounder form in mind.

She should have guessed when Sam had first mentioned it this morning that his team was composed of women. All of them were energetic and athletic, enthusiastic and competitive, and more than a little in love with their coach. Even Margie Blaines, who Laura knew for a fact was happily married and a mother several times over, winked and grinned whenever Sam spoke to her.

Laura didn't mind helping the team out for just this one game. The vacationing members would be back in a couple of days, and she would be off to Washington to get her things. Besides, when Sam had made the suggestion that morning, she had latched on to it like a drowning woman spying a raft. It didn't matter that they had painting to do and that she was still recovering from a bout of malaria. She had been readily amenable to his suggestion because it gave her something to focus on beside the overwhelming emotions she had felt as the result of his kiss.

Remembering it, her eyes flickered guiltily to the sparse grass at her feet. What had possessed her? Probably some kind of crazy chemical reaction.

That kind of closeness wouldn't happen again. Especially now that she knew what to look for. When her heart started pounding like a runaway race horse, when his eyes took on that lambent gleam, when her palms started to sweat and her knees to shake, when his hands, hard from work, but gentle on her skin, reached out—she would run! She flinched, realizing the route her imagination was taking.

She had to stop thinking like this. Only a few days ago they had been total strangers. Besides, except for the ardor of his kiss, she had no indication of his feelings. He had recovered quickly enough that morning, asking her to substitute on his ball team, turning away, helping her clean up the paint she'd spilled, telling her about the Pointers' win/loss record. The spurt of resentment she'd felt at his offhand attitude was completely ridiculous. She should be grateful that at last one of them had exhibited some good sense.

These thoughts spiraled through her mind as they'd been doing all day, even though she knew her self-reprimands should not have been necessary. Her attention was jerked back to the present by the thwack of the ball against the aluminum bat. Laura's gaze snapped up as she straightened, tracking the ball, hoping it wasn't heading for her. She was too rusty at this game to be of much help to the team.

But the ball *was* headed her way. She started to jog forward, her head back as she watched the fat, white sphere reach the top of its arc and begin its descent.

She could tell herself that her reaction to Sam had been pure chemistry or proximity, but it was his coaching voice she listened to as she tried to determine where the ball would drop, his approval she sought when she held out her glove to make the catch.

Disappointment knifed through her when the ball fell short of her glove. But she scrambled after it, grabbed it and heaved it toward second base where another player, quick and light, snatched it from the air and held the runner up. With an apologetic glance at Sam, she returned to her place, took up her stance and vowed to pay closer attention.

She didn't experience any more lapses in the outfield and acquitted herself well with a single and a walk the two times she came up to bat. By a mere run, the Pointers managed to win. Considering she hadn't played in seven years, she was quite pleased. She refused to think about the sore muscles that would be making themselves known the next day.

As she trotted toward the dugout with the other players. Laura automatically sought out Sam.

"I thought you said you couldn't play?" he teased, handing her a can of icy soda as he looked at her approvingly.

Laura accepted the can and held it to her hot face as she whipped off her borrowed hat and fanned herself with it. "I didn't know I still could."

Sam took in the disheveled mop of strawberry-blond curls clinging damply to her forehead and noted the flush in her cheeks. His mouth worked itself into a frown. "Are you all right?"

She flashed a grin. "This is honest perspiration, not fever. I'm fine."

He started to speak again, but she gave him a bright, empty smile and turned away, knowing she had to stick with her resolution to be friendly, but distant. She had forgotten that for a time this morning, but she wouldn't again.

The team members gathered around, thanking her for helping out on such short notice and inviting her to join them at Webster's one and only pizza parlor for a postgame celebration.

When they piled into cars, Laura was careful to ride with Margie Blaines, rather than Sam, who had brought her to the ballpark. She remembered the woman from her childhood summers, because Margie's family had lived up the street from Belle.

Once they were inside the restaurant and pitchers of soda and beer had been ordered, Margie turned to her, smiling.

"I heard Sam ask if you were okay. Did he think you shouldn't be out playing ball a week after your aunt's funeral? He, of all people, should know Belle McCord would have laughed herself hoarse at such a suggestion."

"No. He's the one who invited me." Laura couldn't help the way her gaze strayed down the table to him and she watched him talking and laughing with his team members. "I was sick a couple of days ago." And he had been so helpful, so unusually kind.

Margie read the tender look in Laura's eyes for what it was, and her smile broadened. "Oh? What was wrong?"

Laura explained about her malaria.

"Where did you catch that?"

In response, Laura launched into an explanation of her time in Africa, ending with a description of the village where she had helped distribute supplies sent by the American government. "So many of the people were ill, especially the children," she said, shrugging, and lifting her hands in a helpless gesture. "But I honestly never thought I'd get sick, too. I was laid up with malaria for two weeks, worst bout I've ever had, missed my vacation, and..." Too late, she realized the other people at the table had gone silent, and she glanced up to meet Sam's eyes. They were intense, fixed on her as she faltered, then resumed what she'd been saying. "And, well, I missed my vacation," she finished lamely, wondering what he was thinking. "Fortunately good medical care is available in Dakar."

One of the other women made a comment about the difficulty of recovering from tropical diseases and the conversation shifted to her. Margie turned to listen, and over her head, Laura's eyes were drawn inexorably to Sam's. She read in them a message of approval that she'd rarely seen during their short acquaintance. Though she felt warmed by it, she also felt that she wasn't ready for approval from him. They had been pulling in opposite directions since the moment they met. She wasn't quite prepared for that to change; there had been too many changes in her life already.

She considered this for several seconds until she guiltily became aware that Margie was talking to her. "Belle was so proud of you. Whenever I saw her in town, she would brag about your glamorous career. It must have been exciting, especially living in Paris."

"It certainly was."

Margie's bright eyes widened. "Tell me, did you meet any devastatingly sexy Frenchmen while you were there and have a flaming love affair?"

The women nearest them groaned comically while Laura laughed and shook her head. "No, nothing so exciting. Actually, I dated another member of the embassy staff. We're... engaged." As soon as she said the words, she regretted them. They weren't really true. She and Jason had only vaguely talked of marriage, but it occurred to her now that this was a good way to keep some distance between Sam and herself. She could use Jason as a buffer to keep from falling too heavily under Sam's charismatic spell. "His name is Jason Creed," she added.

Sam must have heard what she said, because he frowned slightly and turned away.

Relieved, yet uncomfortable with her mild deception, Laura forced herself to ask the woman across from her how she'd become interested in playing softball.

After the impromptu celebration, Sam drove Laura home. The truck lurched and protested as much as ever, but it got them across town. Sam didn't say much until they pulled up in front of her house and she started gathering up the cap and glove he had lent her.

"Laura?" His voice was intimate in the cab of the battered, old vehicle.

She looked up to see him watching her intently. "Yes, Sam?"

"The vacation you missed because you were sick—where were you going to go?"

Laura slid over in the seat, reaching for the door handle, forgetting that it was difficult to open from the inside. "That was a year ago. What does it matter now?"

"It matters to me." Her left hand rested on the seat, and he covered it with his own.

She started at the warmth, but didn't pull away.

"Where were you going on your vacation, Laura?"

Her heart filled with some nameless emotion and her lips trembled. It was suddenly of vital importance that he think well of her. "I was coming home to surprise Belle. I had two weeks. She had written that she'd strained her back, so I knew she'd be housebound for that time. I hadn't seen her since she visited me in France when I was assigned there. When someone you love is getting on in years, you want to be with them as much as possible." Her gaze flashed up to him, then away. "Storing memories for the future, you know?"

"I know." He was silent for a long time, his hand shifting so that his fingers could smooth over the ridges of her knuckles.

She wondered if she should tell him about the way Belle had sung his praises, or her own reluctance to come home and meet him. With a flash of insight, she realized part of her reluctance had been caused by guilt. She had felt that she'd neglected her great-aunt and, irrationally, didn't want to meet the man who was doing for Belle all the things she couldn't do herself.

Chagrined, she looked down to where their joined hands were visible in a pool of buttery-yellow brightness coming from the streetlight. Laura watched his fingers, felt their callused roughness against her softness while her mind spilled over with images of him.

"I was wrong, Laura. I'm sorry. I said things I didn't mean and shouldn't have even thought."

She lifted her face, flushed with emotion, and encountered his clear gray eyes, free of any censure. Her own eyes were in shadow and her lips shook as she tried to speak. He had apologized in the most humble voice she had ever heard from him, the most contrite. "I... I'm sorry, too. It seems we've been at odds since we met—"

"Stupid of us," he interrupted. "When both of us loved Belle so much."

Unable to speak past the lump in her throat, Laura simply gazed at him, her eyes full of the words she couldn't say.

"She taught me so much about myself, about life," Sam went on. "When I moved here from

New York, I was bitter. Just wanted to vegetate, but she wouldn't let me."

Laura smiled shakily. "Life is for the living..."

"...so get on with it," he finished softly. The atmosphere in the truck was stifling, steamy hot, darkly intimate.

All the reasons she was attracted to him crowded into Laura's mind—his kindness to Belle, his sense of humor, his integrity, his bone-deep sexiness.

With his free hand, Sam reached up to touch her cheek, sliding his thumb over the faint dusting of freckles on her skin.

Laura wanted to go to him, but she held back. Confusion overwhelmed her. Too much had happened in the past week. She wasn't ready for this. There had been too many changes. She didn't need another one. It frustrated her that she could so easily forget her decision to keep some distance between them.

Breathing erratically Laura drew her hand from beneath his and pressed up against the door, clutching at the handle. Of course it didn't open. "I've uh, got to go...go in, now, Sam." She tried it again, and when it wouldn't budge, she brought the heel of her hand to her forehead in frustration. "Could you please open this damned door?"

The slightly hysterical note in her voice must have reached him, because she heard his breath hiss in. He turned and shouldered his own door open, slid to the ground and came around to open hers. He blocked the way, though, when she tried to get out, and she was forced to look up at him.

"Laura, what...?"

"I'm tired, Sam. I'm not used to this much physical activity, especially after being sick." There, lay some guilt on him, she thought, angry with herself.

His lips compressed as he stepped back. She knew he wanted to pursue the discussion, force her to acknowledge his apology, but she needed some space, some time to sort this out.

With a murmured "Good night," she hurried up the stairs, fumbled with the lock and dashed inside.

Things had been much easier when she had truly disliked him. Now she didn't know how she felt, but she did know that her emotions were becoming far too complicated.

LAURA WAS NERVOUS about seeing Sam the next morning, but he solved the problem by calling to say that Brandy had a sore leg and needed to go to the vet. He promised to be over later and suggested she continue with the painting.

Relieved to be left alone, Laura did as he said, finishing the ornate molding and starting on the baseboards. She hoped to finish that day, partly to show Sam she was just as willing as he was to work on the house, and partly so she could have at least one small accomplishment to her name when she left to take care of business in Washington. There was a bus out of Webster that afternoon and another early the next day to Greenville, where she could catch a plane to Washington. She planned to be ready for the next morning's bus.

She was on her hands and knees, working her way slowly around the room, when she heard the mail drop through the slot in the front door and scatter on the hardwood floor. Deciding it was a good time for a break, she balanced her paintbrush across the top of the can and rose to her feet. She walked, bent over slightly, to the front door, massaging her reddened knees and the muscles in her thighs, sore from yesterday evening's ball game, just as she'd predicted.

Standing in that position, she looked at the pile of mail. With one hand she went on kneading her muscles as she studied the circulars and junk mail, noticed the telephone bill, then zeroed in on a long, somewhat battered envelope covered with postage marks and addressed to her in thick strokes of black ink.

Curious, she picked it up. In the left-hand corner was a small, gummed label printed with Sam's name and address. Her brows shot up as she examined the envelope.

Sam had written to her in Senegal? Obviously it had arrived after she'd left. The address had been crossed out, probably by one of the embassy personnel, and her mother's address printed in. Then that had been blocked over and her mother had written in the Webster address.

Laura chewed her lip as she slipped a paint-flecked nail under the flap and opened the envelope. She tried to imagine the various reasons Sam might have had for writing to her. Given his opinion of her when she'd first arrived, none of them seemed promising.

The letter started out with a rather blunt greeting—Miss Decker, no Dear—and went downhill rapidly from there. In Sam Calhoun's opinion, she was neglectful of her aunt, self-centered and unworthy of the love and regard Belle McCord had for her.

Laura straightened as if someone had caught a handful of her hair and yanked her to attention. A band seemed to wrap itself around her chest and tighten with each line she read.

Sam wrote that he couldn't understand why she hadn't been home to visit her aunt. He even offered to pay her airfare if money was the problem. The tone of the letter was one of utmost contempt. Laura pictured him sitting at the desk or his kitchen table, his gray eyes icy and his face grim as he dashed out word after vituperative word.

By the time she reached the bottom of the page and his arrogant signature, the letter was jumping in front of her eyes and she realized she was trembling. She stuffed the paper back into the envelope, then crumpled the whole thing in her hands and let it fall to the floor. She swept it aside with her bare foot, barely noticing as it skidded against the wall.

She bent over slightly, in a stance similar to the one she'd used the night before on the ball field, and tried to fill her constricted lungs with air. A wave of dizziness swamped her, but she fought it back. She couldn't believe how much his comments hurt her, though she didn't know why she should have been surprised. Sam's feelings about her treatment of Belle certainly weren't a secret. But his accusations, so boldly stated in black and white, hurt more than she could ever have imagined.

Still, he *did* apologize, a part of her argued as she moved like a sleepwalker away from the scattered mail. She sank onto the plastic-swathed sofa, planted her elbows on her bare knees and stared at her hands.

How much of what he had said in the letter did he still believe? Was his change of heart genuine? Laura's hands clenched. Why did it matter so much? Unwilling to consider the answer to that, she stood up, deciding to catch the afternoon bus to Greenville, instead of waiting until the next morning.

In a flurry of activity, she washed her paint-brush, sealed the can of paint and rushed upstairs to take a shower. Within an hour she was dressed in her yellow linen dress and high heels. Her makeup and hair were correct and her suitcase neatly packed.

She hurried down the stairs, which were covered by a worn runner of carpet. Setting the case down, she first called Tully's Taxi to come for her, then Mr. Sweeting, who agreed to feed the cats while she was gone. She knew Sam would have done it, but it was time to start breaking off her obligation to him. While it was true that she would be dependent on him for money, she was going to make sure that was all she needed from him.

Laura took the house key over to Mr. Sweeting, then rushed back home to compose a note to Sam and wait for Tully to arrive. She was pacing the half-painted living room when she heard a knock on the door. Sweeping up her purse and suitcase, she darted to open it, assuming the caller was Tully.

It was Sam. He had a grin on his face and his arms were full of dog. Brandy's normally bright eyes were glazed and his head lolled.

"Hi! Mind if I bring him in? He won't tear the place up because he's still sedated and I..." His gaze skipped over her tight unwelcoming face, down her neat dress and finally rested on the suitcase in her hand. He looked back at her face. "Going somewhere?"

Her chin bobbed in a stiff nod. "To Washington. Right away."

"Some kind of government crisis?" He eased past her to lay the bandaged retriever down in a patch of sun on the living room floor.

"No." She moved away restlessly and glanced out at the empty street, willing Tully to hurry. "I told you I was going to Washington to get my things, and—"

"Why so sudden?" His eyes narrowed beneath his dark, forbidding brows.

"We've already talked about this, and I don't have to answer to you."

"True." His tone was reasonable, but his expression was growing impatient. "But I'd like to know."

"I've wasted enough time here." She refused to meet his eyes. Her back and shoulders shifted, then were straight.

"Wasted?"

She tucked a red-gold curl behind her ear. "Yes, it's time I got on with my life and I'm—"

"Babbling," he interjected, his thick brows drawing together. "What's this all about? I thought we were finally coming to some kind of understanding." He glanced around the room as if searching for any changes that had taken place in his absence. His gaze landed on the mail.

Self-consciously, Laura gathered her skirt and crouched to collect the assorted circulars and bills. She reached for the crumpled letter, but he was there before her and snatched it up.

Straightening, he looked at the scrawled-over addresses for a long moment before lifting his eyes to her. He kept his chin lowered, and the pose made him look ridiculously appealing and vulnerable. "I see this finally arrived. I wondered what had happened to it."

"You could have warned me that you'd written me a poison-pen letter." Hurt spilled over and she bent her head as she turned back to the door, wishing Tully would hurry up.

"I think that's overstating the case somewhat," he said, dropping the letter onto a small table. "I apologized for this last night. I said I was wrong about what I thought of you."

"But the feelings behind those accusations are still there."

He stepped over to her and searched her face. With Laura in high heels, they were eye to eye. "I don't think it's my feelings you're worried about. It's yours. You're running away."

She threw him a look that said such a statement didn't deserve an answer. Avoiding him carefully, she picked up her suitcase and moved out onto the porch. She saw with relief that Tully's cab was just coming up the road. "I've given Mr. Sweeting a key to the house and asked him to feed the cats, so you won't have to bother."

Sam stalked along right behind her. When he spoke again his voice was low and silky. "Oh, it's no bother. I've got to finish the painting, anyway."

Laura's gaze flew to his. "Don't paint everything gray!"

"Why should it matter? After all, you're only staying a year."

Tully pulled up in front of the house. Laura hurried toward the cab. "Oh, damn it! Never mind. Paint it any color you like!"

Sam just stood there and she could feel him watching her as she threw her suitcase into the cab, then followed in a swirl of yellow skirt. She slammed the door and struggled to roll up the window.

"Have a nice trip, Laura," Sam said mockingly. "I'll be waiting right here when you get back."

That was what she was afraid of. A confusing mixture of sorrow and relief washed over her as she told Tully to take her to the bus station. As they drew away, she couldn't resist one last look at Sam.

He still stood on the porch, his arms folded over his chest, his wicked mouth curved in a sardonic grin and his eyes narrowed. She knew he was silently calling her a coward, which was exactly what she was.

WASHINGTON WAS even hotter and steamier than South Carolina. Laura found the apartment she had sublet to be much more modern and soulless than she remembered. Its sleek furniture didn't appeal to her nearly as much as Belle's collection of scarred antiques and reproductions. Still, she dragged out her return to Webster for a full week, visiting the few people she knew in the capital and making trips to her favorite museums. She could have spent a month in the Smithsonian Institution alone. But even the Smithsonian couldn't keep her thoughts from turning to Sam.

She had hoped that a few days away from him would give her time to come to grips with everything that had happened. Now she could think objectively about the delayed letter she'd received from him and recognize that her reaction was based on self-directed guilt. Every accusation he had made was one she had already heaped on her own head. She wondered again how much of it he still believed.

She had no answer, so she dawdled in Washington long after she'd had a stiff little interview with the man who was to have been her boss and told him she wouldn't be taking the job. She could have written a formal letter, but that seemed so impersonal, and she didn't want to burn all her bridges. There was no telling when she'd be job-hunting again, and diplomatic work was all she knew.

She had to return to Webster sometime, though, and she found herself missing the cats. She called Mr. Sweeting twice to check on them and each call made her miss them more.

Something had to be done about her transportation, or lack of it. She went to a car dealer in Virginia and wiped out her savings buying an almost new minivan. She didn't even bother asking about a loan. A woman with no job would have been laughed off the car lot. The purchase meant she had barely enough funds to cover her month's expenses and might have to go to Sam for money sooner than she'd planned, a possibility she abhorred, but one that couldn't be helped.

With her car packed full of the belongings that had arrived miraculously unscathed from Senegal, Laura started out for South Carolina. Leaving the capital, cutting all ties to the job she had so happily anticipated, didn't concern her as much as she'd expected. Belle would have laughed at her and told her she was stuck in a rut, and too intent on her career, anyway. Life was a constantly changing kaleidoscope, and Laura should be taking time to enjoy it. Sam Calhoun would have echoed that sentiment.

Exasperated at the way her thoughts constantly swung back to him, Laura gripped the wheel and concentrated on the highway and on watching Virginia's beautiful green countryside roll by. She took her time, stretching the trip out to a full two days. In spite of paying careful attention to her map, she made several wrong turns and saw more of North Carolina than she had intended. Sam wouldn't have gotten lost, she thought petulantly. He probably would have hopped in the car and ended up exactly where he wanted to be without once consulting the map.

As she drove, she wondered whether she was making a mistake in taking her time on the drive. It gave her too much opportunity to think. And no matter how long she thought, she couldn't reconcile herself to her strange attraction to Sam Calhoun. He was everything she didn't want to be: laid-back, easygoing, apparently without goals.

On the other hand, Jason Creed probably knew exactly where he'd be in five years, ten years, even twenty years. No doubt he fully expected to be the American ambassador to a major world power by the time his youngest child, one of two perfect children, started at an Ivy League university.

Laura shifted uncomfortably on the seat and looked up to meet her own accusing eyes in the mirror. She had led Sam to believe she was seriously interested in Jason; not long ago, set on her career, rigid in her ways, she probably would have married him. The time she'd spent in Webster had brought a richness to her life, a dimension she hadn't even known was lacking. Not a little of this had to do with attractive, maddening Sam Calhoun.

Soon she would have to tell Sam the truth. She knew that if she hadn't been so shaken by Belle's death and the will, and also by her own reaction to Sam, she never would have lied about her relationship with Jason. She sighed, and with a last rueful look in the mirror, returned her attention to her driving.

Laura arrived back in Webster early the next evening. Automatically her gaze flashed up the street to Sam's house. His repaired red Thunderbird was parked in the drive behind his rusty old truck. A sporty, silver compact was parked there, too, telling her he had visitors, or maybe just one visitor. Perhaps one of the smitten members of his softball team.

Irritated that she even cared, Laura looked at her own house and saw Sam standing on the front porch, watching her approach. His hands rested lightly on his lean waist. As always, he was dressed in faded jeans and T-shirt.

For a wild instant she thought he had been waiting there for her for the past ten days. Unbidden joy capered through her before she could subdue it.

As she braked slowly, he crossed his arms over his chest. A frown curved lines into his forehead.

Laura had a moment's crazy wish that he would trot down the stairs and fold her into his arms, welcoming her home. She mentally shook herself, furious that she found the idea so appealing.

She had stopped the car with the passenger side toward him. She slowly stepped down from the high seat and adjusted the pleated legs of her khaki shorts. She tugged her purse from the tumble of maps, fast-food bags and shoes that had collected on the passenger seat. When she felt ready, she took a deep breath and rounded the car to face him.

He sauntered down the front steps. His eyes flicked over her and she thought she saw relief there, but then he smiled coolly. "Decided to come back, hmm?"

"There was never any doubt."

"Maybe not for you."

"Does this mean you've been thinking about me?" Her brows rose. "That's very flattering."

He shrugged. "Not me, but your fiancé has."

It took her a moment to realize whom he meant. "Jason?"

"He's called here three times. Gets pretty ticked off whenever I answer."

She pinched her lips tightly together. "What have you said to him, Sam?"

"Told him you were busy. When's the big wedding?" he asked, rocking nonchalantly back on his heels. "I'll need to get my white tie and tails out of the pawnshop."

Laura ignored that bit of idiocy. "You mean you didn't let him know I was in Washington?"

"Why? You didn't have a phone there, did you?"

Her hands clenched. She was quickly losing her temper again. "That's not the point. You could have at least told him..." She paused, realizing that she was delving deeper and deeper into an argument with him, which was probably just what he wanted.

Maybe she could provoke him to anger so they could have a rousing free-for-all that would clear the air and permanently destroy the sexual awareness sparking between them. Closing her eyes she counted slowly to three. Finally she managed to speak calmly. "Did you finish painting?"

His gray eyes blinked at her change of subject, then he smiled, a slow-breaking, slanted smile that kicked her traitorous heart into overdrive. "No. I decided you were right. You should be the one to pick out the colors. We can go to the hardware store tomorrow. You pick. I'll pay."

Her nose wrinkled as if she'd sniffed something rotten. Now what was he up to? "All right," she said, her voice tinged with caution. "And...and while we're on the subject of money, I need some."

Sam's mouth stretched into a full-blown grin, but before he could answer, another male voice interrupted from behind his shoulder.

"A woman asking for money. Lord, Sam, I thought you'd reformed."

"We'd better call Mom," another voice added. "Let's just hope they make it legal before the baby comes."

CHAPTER EIGHT

SAM WHIPPED his head around to glance over his shoulder. Laura was glad his eyes were no longer on her, because she was blushing all the way up to her hairline.

She watched as two young men walked across her porch and down the steps to join Sam. They were as tall as he was, but one was blond and the other had hair halfway between that shade and Sam's sable brown. When she looked into their amused eyes, she knew immediately that they were Sam's brothers.

"Will, no one is interested in your brand of juvenile humor," Sam said, giving the brown-haired man a long-suffering grimace.

"I am," the other one said, shouldering Sam aside to take Laura's limp hand and pump it industriously. "Hi, I'm Bret Calhoun, and this is my brother, Will. We came by to make Sam's life miserable . . ."

"And doing a damned fine job of it," Sam muttered, reaching over pointedly to catch

Laura's wrist and pluck it from his brother's grip.

"...and to meet the woman who's got him hanging out of windows, watching the road."

"Bret!"

"Uh-oh, little brother, you're making him mad. He's gonna give us another one of those for-our-own-good lectures he likes so much." Will came forward, his gray eyes warm and laughing, to take Laura's hand from Sam's grasp. He jerked his chin at Bret. "Go find a pencil and paper. If we take notes on his lecture this time, maybe we can skip the next one."

Bret made a very succinct suggestion about where Will could go with his idea and Will laughed.

Dazed by the overwhelming presence of not one, but three Calhoun men, Laura opened and closed her mouth a couple of times.

"See there?" Sam asked. His eyelids drooped lazily, but they didn't hide the sharp gleam. "She's so appalled by the two of you, she can't find words to express her condolences to me."

The two of them continued to razz him, but Sam ignored them and took Laura's arm. "As they said, these are my brothers—Will, who fancies himself an artist, though he's in his last year at Vanderbilt University, and Bret, who's a reporter for a Memphis newspaper. They came over tonight to help me finish painting your ceilings. They'd been sitting around my place eating me out of house and home for three days, until I decided it was time for them to start earning their keep."

Laura finally found her voice and held out her hand, smiling as the two men made faces at their older brother. "I'm Laura Decker and I'm glad to meet you."

"You don't have to be polite to them, Laura. It'll only encourage them."

Bret manufactured an innocent look. "Oh, we don't need any encouragement." His gaze skimmed over her, his eyes glinting appreciatively. "I know we've just met, but will you marry me?"

Laura burst out laughing.

"Damn it, Bret!" Irritated, Sam grabbed the keys she still held and shoved them at his brother. "You guys make yourselves useful and unload her car. She and I have some business to discuss."

Will winked, then wiggled his thick Calhoun eyebrows lecherously. "Is it what Mom would call monkey business?"

"Get moving." Sam pointed to the minivan. He took her arm again. "Ignore them. They were dropped on their heads in infancy."

"By you!" Will shot back. Then he and Bret strode cheerfully to the van and started pulling out boxes and bags while Sam led her up the porch steps.

"Sorry about that," he said once they were inside. He let go of her, but the warmth of his touch stayed behind.

Unconsciously Laura rubbed her elbow. If she hung around the three Calhoun brothers very long she'd have one arm dragging along the ground like a chimpanzee's! They certainly weren't standoffish.

Her face lighting with amusement, Laura held up her hands. "Don't worry about it. God made siblings to keep the oldest child humble."

"Well, in that case, I'm ready for sainthood," he muttered, his glance lingering on the froth of curls around her face, the dusting of freckles on her nose, and finally settling on her mouth. "You took longer in Washington than I thought you would."

Her lips tingled as if he'd touched them and her heart raced before idling back to its regular speed. Her throat worked for a moment before she could speak. "I had things to take care of."

"Like buying a car?"

The censorious tone in his voice shattered her absorption with him. She had been foolishly staring into his face, hoping for some sign of greeting, some sign that he'd missed her. It was more than obvious that he hadn't. "That's right."

Turning in the entryway, she looked around the front of the house, then into the dining room. The ceilings had, indeed, been finished, in a pure, alpine white. "This looks fine, Sam." Actually it looked great, but she refused to say so, then silently berated herself for being petty.

He ignored her attempt to change the subject. "And now you're out of money."

Darn it, she thought. She could have pummeled him for his indulgent tone. "Yes," she answered, lifting her chin and daring him to make fun of her.

"What did you do? Pay cash?"

Her eyes widened and she looked at him as if he had taken leave of his senses. "Of course. I couldn't get a loan, since I have no job!"

"Any car dealer would have arranged things if you'd told them you'd recently inherited a fortune. Then you could have called me to take the money out of Belle's trust account and deposit it in yours."

"I didn't want to come to you. Besides, the car was for me."

One corner of his mouth edged up. "But you had to come to me, anyway. You know that Belle didn't have a car because she didn't trust her eyesight anymore, but there was certainly enough money for one.''

"I didn't want to be indebted to you for transportation." He was enjoying this, she thought, anger and embarrassment heating her face. "Or anything else."

The amusement drained from his craggy features as if a plug had been pulled. He reached up tiredly and rubbed the back of his neck. "You've made that abundantly clear." Hearing his brothers coming, he went to hold the door.

Still upset, Laura directed Will and Bret to put her things in the dining room. Amid good-natured grumbling, they piled everything in a corner and went back for the rest. Within minutes they'd unloaded the van and Will was clearing it of her accumulated trash.

"This is my kind of woman," he said, holding up an empty fast-food bag. "A cheap date."

"Cut it out, Will," Sam snapped with far more force than the mild teasing warranted. "And let's get going. I want to check on the dogs before it's completely dark."

The brothers exchanged looks. They mouthed "wow" at each other and Bret said, "As if those kennels didn't have the latest in lighting."

Laura knew why Sam wanted to go. He was anxious to get away from her. She wished she could convince herself that she felt the same. In spite of the wild upheavals in her life and the decision she had made to keep her distance from Sam, she was glad to see him and reluctant for him to go. She tried to keep the sadness from her face and voice as she told his brothers good-night.

With silly protestations of undying love, the two younger men left.

Sam followed, then turned back to her. "I've decided you were right about the paint," he said gruffly. "You need to help pick it out. We'll go to the hardware store first thing in the morning."

Before Laura could remind him that he had already told her that, he stalked out. Wondering what had brought about his change of mind, she closed the door behind him, clicked the lock and walked wearily into the sun-room to see the cats. They greeted her with their usual condescending air and Laura smiled as the peacefulness of the familiar house wrapped itself around her.

Mr. Sweeting must have been doing an especially good job of feeding the cats. Guinevere was fatter than ever. Concerned, Laura ran her hands over her. If this continued, she was going to have to take her to the vet for a checkup. There might be something seriously wrong. She turned the cat's face toward her and saw that her eyes were clear, though sleepy, and she was purring contentedly.

After spending a few minutes with them, she went into the dining room to find the suitcase in which she'd packed her necessities for the night. She hefted it and started for the stairs.

Now her year was really beginning, she told herself, placing one hand on the burled maple banister. When the time was up, she could go back to Washington, to a new job, to new friends, to her old, exciting way of life. Somehow the idea held less and less appeal.

THE CALHOUN BROTHERS showed up the next morning to take her to the hardware store. Will and Bret were laughing and teasing, heartily approving of the cutoffs and snug white T-shirt she wore, but Sam's expression was that of a man with a dead fish for a tie. "Remind me never to invite my brothers to visit again," he muttered.

Laura blinked in surprise at his tone, wondering what had prompted it. She would have liked to think he wanted time alone with her, but then dismissed the idea.

She insisted on driving them in her new minivan. And when they arrived at the store, she received a great deal more advice on color selections than she needed. Her paint choices ran to pastels, and she imagined the rooms of the big old house artistically decorated, with the antique furniture and maple floors gleaming. Fancy dreams for someone who planned to sell the house, she acknowledged, with a guilty look at Sam.

Back at her house, Sam and Bret immediately started painting the living room in the pale peach she had chosen. She was grateful that Sam had decided to save the gray paint for some future project of his own—painting a battleship, perhaps. Laura objected to letting Will and Bret do all the painting, though, saying she ought to hire a contractor.

Sam gave her an appalled look. "These guys are going to be here for another week. I've got to keep them busy. Besides, Will needs an outlet for his artistic creativity."

Laura looked around at the buckets of paint, plastic drop cloths and rollers with long extensions. "Oh, this should qualify as artistic, all right."

Will started picking up supplies. "Don't worry about it, Laura. Every true creator has to suffer for his art. Let's get started in the dining room."

She knew that Sam was watching her as she followed his brother across the front hall and into the other room. Frowning a little, Laura opened cans of the powder-blue paint she had chosen to complement her great-aunt's collection of Wedgewood china that stood on railed shelves around the top of the wall. Her face fell as she realized that in a year's time she'd be taking the pieces down, probably storing them until she had an appropriate place for them in some future home of her own. Maybe Sam was right. Maybe she should have painted the entire inside of the house in drab grey and left it at that. It might have made the idea of staying there permanently less attractive.

Will must have caught her look as he turned from wrestling the cherrywood sideboard out of the corner. "Hey, don't let him worry you," he said, pushing his light brown hair back from his forehead.

She blinked. "Who?"

"Sam. Don't let him bother you. He's a grouch sometimes, but believe me, he's a hell of a lot better than he was when his wife dumped him and almost bankrupted him."

Wife? She turned so swiftly, her knee struck the paint can, almost capsizing it. Her hands shot out to steady it. "Dumped him? Bankrupted him?" Her mind raced over the sketchy details Sam had given of his life. He had mentioned the brokerage house, but never anything about a wife!

Absorbed in removing the pictures and their nails from the walls and filling the holes, Will didn't seem to hear the surprise in her voice. "He was sure caught up in the whole corporate life. Spent fourteen hours a day building his business."

Laura knew she probably shouldn't be listening to this, but she couldn't help herself. Apparently Will thought she and Sam knew each other much better than they really did. "Must have been tough," she said casually.

Will shut the door and began searching around it for places to patch and smooth. "Yeah. Lord, he was rich. Who would have guessed a loophole would let Myra have it all?"

Myra? So that was her name. "What she did just showed she had no conscience," Laura agreed, keeping her tone even.

"Had a great pair of legs, though." Will flashed her a lady-killer grin. "That's one thing my big brother can always pick out."

Laura smiled weakly, but her arms felt heavy as she began stirring the paint. ''He must have been terribly hurt.''

''Yeah, but I guess it happens all the time. In a divorce, things never come out equal. Especially when the spouse is also the business partner.''

Sam had been married. A swift icicle of jealousy stabbed through her. Laura waited for it to dissolve, knowing she was being ridiculous. She had no right whatsoever to be jealous. But she was.

''She got half the proceeds of the business, anyway,'' Will continued as he slapped white filler on the walls and smoothed it with the tip of a putty knife. ''So Sam just sold her his half and moved down here. He'd bought the house next door in some kind of bailout of the savings-and-loan that held the mortgage. We were all pretty worried about him. Thought he was going to take up a new career as a hermit.''

Belle had said he was mad at the world. Now Laura knew why.

''We were grateful to your aunt for watching out for him. She pestered the daylights out of him until he showed an interest in life again. Dragged him to all kinds of community affairs, got him involved.''

Life is for living, so get on with it. Again, Laura thought about her aunt's epitaph as she continued stirring. What Will had said gave her new insight into Sam's relationship with Belle. It also explained his reaction to her. When she didn't visit Belle and showed up just in time to inherit, he probably thought she was like his ex-wife. And Belle's insistence that he handle the trust account had probably convinced him that she was money-hungry. The whole scenario made his attitude more understandable, if not forgivable.

But she *had* forgiven him, she realized, still stirring. And her feelings for him had gone way beyond forgiveness.

"Do you plan to turn that stuff into whipped cream?" Will asked, standing over her. "Or could we maybe slap a little on the walls before it congeals?"

Startled, Laura looked down to see that she had been stirring so vigorously that the paint had pooled around the rim of the can and splashed down the outside. "Oh, of course." Embarrassed, she ducked her head as she poured some of the blue liquid into the paint tray and handed it to him. She took the can and a small brush and began covering the corners and edges where the roller couldn't reach.

The two of them worked well together and finished the dining room just about the time Sam and Bret finished the living room. They broke for lunch and painted two more rooms that afternoon. For the first time, Laura got excited as she imagined the house all fixed up. But her energy began to lag by midafternoon, so the brothers Calhoun nudged her out of the way, sending her off to take a nap with the cats, while they continued working. She went gratefully, promising she would cook dinner for them that night.

Content, she lowered the shades in the sunroom and curled up on the window seat, with Guinevere at her feet and Percival cradled against her stomach. It was a hot arrangement for the sultry afternoon, but she was happy to have them near. The other five cats were ranged about the room, playing with their toys or sleeping. Smiling, she drifted off.

Something brushed her face and she reached up, still half-asleep, to touch it. Her slim fingers curled around the object, which was warm and solid and nestled against her cheek. She kept her eyes closed, trying to identify its familiar shape and texture. It was a hand, she decided. Laura tugged, and it eased around willingly. The faintly bitter smell of latex-based paint greeted her, along with...Aunt Belle's powder? Impossible.

Jolted, Laura opened her eyes to see Sam hovering over her, smiling in his sweetly crooked way. He was kneeling beside the window seat, so his face was level with hers. Barely moving, he leaned forward, his face filling her vision, his lips sighing open.

Some fragment of self-preservation started her fully awake as if a slamming door had rattled the house. Laura shot up so fast her head struck Sam's cheek.

Guinevere and Percival bolted across the room and stared at her in disgust from the back of a chair.

"Ow!" Sam fell backward onto the floor and slapped a hand up to his face. "Watch it, will you?"

Defensive, she said, "Why don't you? What were you doing, anyway?" Stupid question. She knew exactly what he was doing—assaulting her senses, making her want him.

"I was just trying to wake you up. It's a scientific fact that if you touch someone's ear gently, they'll wake up without being surprised."

She swung her feet to the floor and shoved paint-stained fingers through her hair, nervously trying to smooth it. "Well, you're no scientist."

He stood up in one easy motion and towered over her. "I didn't expect you to start making love to my hand!"

Hot color flamed into her face. "I was not—"

"Now, children!" Will said as he and Bret bumped together in the doorway to see what all the shouting was about. "Let's have none of that, or you'll have to settle the argument the way Sam used to make us settle one."

"Shut up, Will," Sam growled, flicking a killing glance toward his brother.

Trying to muster some dignity, Laura rose and moved away from Sam. "How's that?"

"He made us kiss and make up. Having to kiss each other was so disgusting that we always forgot the argument by the time we got around to the kiss."

Bret elbowed his older brother. "I don't think these two would mind kissing and making up."

"You're wrong," Laura said primly. "I would!"

Sam's thick lashes lowered. "Liar," he muttered in a voice too low for his brothers to hear.

She ignored him, knowing he was right and hating him for it. "I have to go to the market before I can cook dinner. Be back in an hour and a half, if you're hungry."

"*If* we're hungry," Will and Bret exclaimed. "We've been painting your house!"

"She's giving us our walking papers, guys," Sam observed sardonically. He headed for the outside door. "Come on. Let's go turn the dogs out for an hour or so. They need the exercise."

"All right," Will said, trudging along. "But doesn't anyone ever get any rest around here?"

"You can catch up on your sleep by snoring through next semester's classes," Bret promised. "Like you did last year."

Laura watched them go, then locked the door after them and hurried upstairs for her purse. On the way, she noticed the rooms that had been painted, pleased with their clean freshness. Unfortunately each room had huge stacks of furniture and other things piled in the middle. She'd have to clear everything out before she could refinish the floors. Sam would probably want to help her.

She heartily wished he wasn't taking his promise to Belle quite so seriously and wasn't around so much. He had been right about her wanting a kiss. She'd been all but begging him. More and more he was in her thoughts and, heaven help her, apparently in her dreams!

As PROMISED, the Calhouns were back an hour later, scrubbed clean and ready to eat. At McFee's grocery, Laura had put one chicken in her basket, thought about their probable appetites and added two more. She now had two pans of meaty chicken parts frying and a huge pot of potatoes ready to be whipped with butter and milk. She knew it was too hot for such a heavy meal, but she also knew that weather made no difference to male appetites.

The kitchen was becoming unbearably hot, with the stove adding to the buildup of heat. Her face shone with perspiration and her hair clustered on her forehead in damp ringlets. She turned the chicken pieces over, covered the pans, and headed to the refrigerator for some iced tea.

"It smells great in here," Will observed, striding in, followed by Bret and Sam.

She turned to smile at them, and her attention was instantly caught by Sam. He was dressed in new jeans and a bright blue cotton shirt that picked up the color of his eyes and turned them the shade of the sky at midday. Pleasure zinged through her and must have shown in her face, because he stopped short, his face intent, before he continued into the room.

Flustered, Laura set her frosty glass down and started to lift the heavy pot of potatoes to the sink.

"Let me do that," Sam offered, removing her hand and wrapping his own around the pot holders she'd covered the handle with.

Laura could feel his warmth against her back and she turned to look up into his eyes, then at his lips, thinking how close she had come to kissing him only a short time ago. Those lips stretched into a knowing smile. Laura cleared her throat. "Oh, yes, thank you."

With his brothers watching as if they'd just come upon the world's greatest stage play, Sam carried the pot to the sink and drained the starchy water out. Will and Bret swung their faces toward her to see what she'd do next, but she simply turned the chicken pieces yet again with a long fork.

Will volunteered to toss a salad, and Bret set the kitchen table. The awkward moment between Sam and Laura passed, and by the time they sat down to eat, the four of them were chatting like old friends.

Will and Bret raved about her cooking, swearing her in as an honorary member of the family right then and there. Will was on the verge of proposing marriage, a chicken leg clutched to his heart, when the phone rang.

Since Sam was closest, he leaned back in his chair and scooped up the receiver. "Calhoun here," he answered, his eyes on Laura. "Oh, hello, Jason, old buddy. How are you?"

Laura reached out a hand. "Sam, give me that!"

"Yes, I gave her your messages. If she chooses not to call you back, that's her business."

Laura shot up as if ejected from her chair by a spring. "Sam!" She hurried around the table and wrestled the receiver from him. He pretended surprise and offense as he surrendered it.

"...and what's more, you have no right to even be in her house," Jason was squawking as she broke in.

"Jason, it's Laura. I just got home last night, or I would have called."

"Well, really, I don't know why it's always so hard to track you down. Not to mention expensive. Is it to much too expect a little consideration?"

She flashed a look at Sam, who smirked in return. "Well, no, of course not, but—"

"And why is that guy always at your house? You're not living with him, are you?"

"Jason!" Her shock must have reverberated all the way across the Atlantic Ocean. "Of course not!"

The Calhouns sat forward, listening shamelessly.

"Wow," Will said, rolling his gray eyes heavenward. "I haven't seen this much drama since Bret broke up with his last girlfriend."

Irritated, Laura turned and, dragging the receiver's long cord, went into the sun-room. She kicked the door shut. Stretching the cord to its full length, she moved far from the door and spoke furiously. "I think you owe me an apology, Jason."

He sighed and she could just imagine him running his hand over his hair to make sure it was neat. "I'm sorry, Laura, but I've been worried about you."

Partially mollified, she told him where she had been and about the work she was doing on the house.

"Hey, that's great," Jason approved. "You'll be able to get a better price for it if it's all fixed up. Cosmetic improvements can really jack up the value."

She had thought so, too, but didn't like hearing Jason putting words to it. Disconcerted by her own hypocrisy, she mouthed some trite answer.

"But I want to know about that guy who keeps answering the phone. What's he doing there?"

Destroying her piece of mind. "Well, he was a good friend of Aunt Belle's, and—"

"You're letting him hang around out of gratitude. Get rid of the guy. He's a freeloader."

"He is not! He's done most of the work on this place and he took care of me when I was sick." Of course that opened up another topic and Laura had to tell Jason about her bout with malaria.

He sympathized and then said, "Laura, Calhoun made a comment the other day on the phone that surprised me."

Laura's heart seemed to jump into her throat. "Oh?" she asked faintly. "What?"

"He seems to think we're ready to set a date. I know we've talked about marriage, but I thought we were going to wait until I was back in the States."

She winced. Her deception was coming back on her own head, and she knew she deserved whatever happened. "Listen, Jason, I can explain—"

"No need," he broke in smoothly. "It's probably time we made a definite commitment, although I admit you've taken me by surprise."

Laura's panicked gaze flew around the cozy sun-room as she tried to think of the right way to explain. "Wait a minute, Jason—"

"You've got a year to plan. We could have a really spectacular wedding, invite people who can do us some good in our careers."

This was getting out of control. Laura gripped the phone as she listened and tried to break into his stream of words. "There's something I need to tell you—"

"I'm afraid it'll have to wait," he said. "I've got to go, but I'll be in touch soon. Start making plans." He hung up, leaving her feeling frustrated. She slapped the receiver against her palm, knowing that her real frustration was with herself. In her attempt to throw up a barrier to keep sexy, disturbing Sam at arm's length, she had made a mess of everything. She was going to have to explain to both Sam and Jason. But how? Sam would think she was foolish—as well as neglectful of her aunt and eager for the inheritance.

Pressing a hand to her knotted stomach, she tried to compose herself before reentering the kitchen.

As she hung up the receiver, she sought out Sam. He was bullying his brothers into cleaning up the kitchen.

He stopped and looked at her, his eyes full of questioning challenge.

Casting him a harried glance, she fled into the dining room, but he caught up with her. "You and the fiancé counting the money you're going to have in a year?"

Laura whirled on him, her golden eyes flashing fire. She could have denied it, but the superior, knowing look on Sam's face, coupled with her own guilt, goaded her. "Not that it's any of your business, but yes, we were!" Turning, she ran up the stairs and slammed her bedroom door.

CHAPTER NINE

WILL AND BRET stayed for a week full of laughter and fun, making Laura homesick for the chaos of her own family in Alaska. Sam seemed to tolerate his brothers with a combination of affection and exasperation.

She had considered Sam to be laid-back and easygoing, but the two younger Calhouns were much more so. Despite Sam's teasing about Will pretending to be an artist, he proudly told Laura that Will's oil paintings had been featured in gallery exhibitions. Bret talked about his job as a newspaper reporter; from the way he asked questions and watched her and Sam, Laura had no doubt he was good at it.

During their visit, the Calhouns finished painting the inside of Laura's house in the soft colors she had chosen.

When Will and Bret finally left—again with affirmations of undying love for Laura—she was sorry to see them go. They had been a welcome distraction, as well as a buffer between her and their difficult brother. Also, with them around, she had less time to worry about the explanations she needed to make to Sam—and Jason, whom she'd tried to phone without success.

She kept herself as busy as possible looking after the cats, hovering in the backyard whenever they were outside. She didn't want a repeat of the Brandy episode.

Except for Guinevere, who the veterinarian said was too old for motherhood, Laura took the cats in for spaying and neutering.

Mr. Sweeting had approached her about working as a literacy volunteer, teaching adults to read, and she had thought it a wonderful idea. She was to start her training soon.

A friend of Belle's called to ask if she would be interested in taking over her aunt's old spot with the hospital auxiliary, and Laura had agreed. Within days she was helping register people for a health fair. She spent several afternoons reading endless Dr. Seuss books to a six-year-old who was hospitalized with a broken leg. Although it had never seemed important before, she now savored the idea of being a real part of the Webster community, at least for the year she would be in town.

The only drawback was that, more and more, she found living next door to Sam daunting. She was aware of everything he did.

She caught herself opening the sun-room windows and listening to his voice as he called to his dogs and trained the pups. When he played his country music and sang along, she joined him as she worked inside her own house. Several nights a week she saw him drive away in his repaired and repainted car, wearing his team uniform. He had invited her to come watch any of the Pointers' games, but she hadn't done so, knowing she would be tempting fate. Once she had heard what sounded like a train whistle moaning in the distance, and he had rushed from his house like a scalded cat, leapt into his truck and roared away. She'd meant to ask him about that, but then it had slipped her mind.

Her mind conjured up images of what living next door to him for the rest of the year could be like—preparing for holidays, weathering rain and ice storms, running in and out of each other's house, depending on each other as neighbors were supposed to. She could just imagine herself coming to depend on him even more. Although her heart raced at the thought, she saw only trouble ahead.

Now that the interior of the house was painted, she decided to go through everything Belle had collected during her life, sort it, save some things and toss the rest. When that was done, Sam would help her refinish the floors. Then all she would have to do was wait out the remainder of her year there.

Because she knew she couldn't face the atticful of articles from her childhood quite yet, Laura started in Belle's office, a small room at the back of the house, which held only a rolltop desk, a chair, and a four-drawer file cabinet stuffed to the seams with papers. She let the cats roam the house, turned on the overhead fan and sneezed her way through the dust that had accumulated on a lifetime's worth of paper.

She had almost worked her way through the second drawer of the file cabinet when she came upon a folder of her father's school report cards. The teacher's comments, written in fading blue ink, held her enthralled, and she began to get a picture of the man she'd never known as a scrappy little redhead who had spent more than his share of time in the principal's office.

Laura chuckled softly. He must have been a handful for his maiden aunt.

"What's so funny?"

Startled, Laura looked up to see Sam lounging in the doorway, holding one cat and letting another inspect his ankles.

Without warning, the impact of his masculinity slammed into her senses—the way he leaned with one broad shoulder against the doorjamb, the way his flat stomach disappeared into the snug waistband of his worn jeans, the length of his legs.

The sensations brought on by his unexpected appearance whizzed through her and sent her heart dancing in giddy spirals. She could hear the sound of denim whispering along wood as he crouched, put down the black cat he held and ran his hand over the back of the gray half-Siamese.

"Laura? Something wrong?" His forehead was creased with lines of concern.

She snapped herself to attention and swallowed rapidly. Good Lord, she'd been practically salivating over him! "Nothing," she said too brightly, her glance ricocheting off him and back to the papers in her lap. "Why don't you ever knock when you come over here?"

Humor lit his eyes. "I did, but you must not have heard because you were so involved with that." He pointed at the papers in her hand.

Laura considered telling him that most people would just go away if there was no answer to a knock, but she knew better than anybody that Sam wasn't most people. "I came across my father's old school records, so I was reading through them, trying to decide if I should keep them. Did you need something?"

Sam looked down at the cat, then lifted his eyes to Laura. "Yes. The Pointers are finishing their season tonight. We're having an end-of-season party at my house, and the team wanted you to come."

"Really?" Flattered, she straightened eagerly. The women on the team had been fun, the type of people she wanted for friends.

"Really." Sam smiled as he watched her fair skin flush with pleasure. "They told me to invite you myself."

Happiness shone from her eyes and arched the corners of her mouth skyward. "I'd love to. What can I bring?"

The friendly expression on Sam's face warmed her like sunlight piercing through thunderheads. His eyes were fixed on hers as he slowly shook his head. "Not a thing. I'm having it catered. The Pointers won twelve out of eighteen games. Better than last year."

"You're a good coach." Laura's hands were motionless in her lap; his were lovingly stroking the cat he now held against his shoulder.

The room's atmosphere was cozy, and it occurred in some far-off corner of Laura's mind that she should beware. She had gotten herself into a mess by not being completely honest with him. Besides, she had promised herself several times lately that she would keep her distance. Unfortunately he made it darn near impossible. She took a deep breath and glanced down once again at the file in her hands. "Where did you find a caterer in a town this size?"

His brows rose. "We may not be Washington, D.C., but we do have some advantages. A couple of local ladies cater special occasions. Don't worry, you'll like it."

Her mouth firmed. "Why don't you stop taking digs at me?"

The mood between them shattered, he set the cat on its feet and rose. "But you're such a good target."

Turning away, she pulled another file from the drawer. "Oh, go chase your dogs, Sam."

With a wicked chuckle, he disappeared.

Laura flipped open the file in her lap, saw that it was paid bills from the early seventies, dumped it into the rapidly filling trash can and reached back into the drawer. She was going to have to insist that he start knocking before entering her house—to give her a chance to brace herself for his presence, if nothing else!

That night she dressed in a halter-backed sundress of apricot cotton eyelet, took extra care with her hair and makeup and landed on Sam's doorstep with her heart fluttering. For once, she didn't even try to deny that she was dressing to be attractive to him. She figured she'd be safe with all those other women around, looking gorgeous.

After she knocked, she nervously pressed her hand to her cartwheeling stomach, anxious for her first sight of the interior of Sam's house. He flung open the door and for one still moment they regarded each other in a breathless hush of appreciation. He was wearing his uniform shirt, the cotton snug on his biceps and tucked into the ever-present jeans. His gaze slicked over her and came back to her face.

Laura's mouth hung slack for an instant before she snapped it shut. "Hi," she finally said.

The smile he blessed her with was long and slow. "Hi. Come in. Everyone's arrived."

He stepped back and motioned her into his living room, which she discovered was plain but comfortable, with refinished oak floors, scattered dhurrie rugs and overstuffed furniture. It was also full of his uniformed team members and their casually dressed husbands and boyfriends. With a sinking heart, Laura realized she was going to look as out of place in her party dress as a peacock at a sparrow convention.

She didn't have time to dwell on it, though, because Sam was drawing her forward, engaging her in conversation, making her welcome. Laura was immediately surrounded by women who asked about her trip to Washington and commiserated over the difficulty of moving.

The evening was more fun than any embassy function she could remember. She didn't have to worry about the details, such as whether the kitchen had prepared enough food, or if the spouse of some embassy luminary was likely to drink too much and go for a swim in the punch bowl. For several hours she could simply sit back and enjoy herself.

Sam came by to check on her frequently, touching her arm to get her attention, then leaning over her with concern in his eyes to ask how she was doing. She welcomed him with sparkling looks and smiles.

When some of the guests started to leave, citing baby-sitters and work the next day, Laura headed for the door, too. Sam met her there with an alarmed look in his eyes.

"You're not going yet, are you?"

"Well, I—"

"Stay. I'll walk you home in a little while."

Melting beneath the warmth in his eyes, Laura let herself be persuaded.

When the last guest had departed, congratulating Sam on the Pointers' season, he shut the door and looked at her with a grin. "Another successful season comes to a close."

"You must be proud of them." When he stepped nearer, she turned uncertainly to gesture toward the mess on the trestle table in his dining room, then to the glasses and plates scattered around the living room. "Do you want some help cleaning this up?"

"No, I paid the caterers extra to do it. Come on, I'll walk you home."

He ushered her outside with a hand at the small of her back, then took her arm as if they were starting on a long trek, rather than just strolling next door.

The touch of his hand on the soft flesh inside her elbow sent tiny thrills through her, pimpling her arms with gooseflesh. She shivered.

"Hey, how can you be cold in this weather?" Sam's face shone blue-white in the moonglow as he turned to inspect her. When he placed his arm around her shoulders, Laura nearly stumbled. "You're not having another bout of malaria, are you?" he asked anxiously, his fingers brushing her forehead.

"No, uh, that is . . . no." She was certainly experiencing some kind of fever, but it wasn't malaria! Hazily she was aware of his hand against her cheek. Her own trembling fingers lifted to push it away, but lingered, resting against the back of his large, work-roughened hand. Like a woman going down for the third time, she scrambled for something to hold on to. "Uh, I forgot to leave a light on," she murmured. Under the porch roof, she couldn't discern his features.

Sam's breath caressed her face. "It's probably just as well." His fingers delved into the curls at the back of her head and urged her forward into the kiss she'd been afraid would happen, and afraid wouldn't. His lips were open, soft and inviting, and she could no more have kept her own closed against him than she could have stilled the wild pounding of her heart.

She had thought about this for weeks, thought about the way he tasted, felt, smelled. In the center of her dreams Sam had been there, his clever mouth persuading her to do things she shouldn't even consider. But the reality was far better than her memory or even her fantasies.

Sam lifted his other hand to cradle her head as if she was a chalice from which he must drink, or perish. His throat worked in tiny moans of pleasure that only fueled the desire rushing through her like a prairie fire. Had anyone ever kissed her with such ardor? Such passion? No one. Certainly not Jason.

When they drew apart, his eyes glittered like splinters of glass beneath his heavy brows. His hands, still bracing her neck, shook her with gentle force. "You're not really going to marry that Creed guy, are you? Be sensible!"

How could she be sensible with her pulses galloping like this? She licked her lips. "I'm not... That is, we've known each other a long time. We'd talked about marriage... tentatively, you know, but I've been trying to tell him..."

His hands dropped to clasp her shoulders, growing hot on her bare skin. "Tell him what? I don't think you understand that he's only interested in the money you're supposed to inherit." A curse sizzled through the air before he pulled her closer and kissed her again.

This time it wasn't just full of wanting and need, it was savage, demanding a response from her. She couldn't prevent her arms from circling his shoulders, hugging him tightly as she tried to keep from falling. Sam tore his mouth away and trailed kisses down her throat, then began nibbling, persuasively, on her ear. "You thought I wanted Belle's money and hated me for it," he whispered.

"I didn't—"

His fingers dug into her shoulders as he shook her. "Don't lie! You thought I wanted it, even though that wasn't true. But you're willing to marry a man who really wants it. Tell me, did he commit himself to marriage before or after he found out about Belle's will?"

Incensed, Laura twisted out of his arms. "You have no right to ask me that!"

"Why not, when you respond to me the way you do?"

"Why not?" She inched away from him. She was finally emerging from the sensual fog with which he'd surrounded her. Anger and hurt rushed in to replace it. "Because as far as I can tell, you're offering me nothing in return."

"What kind of offer do you want, Laura? If I even tentatively discussed the possibility of marriage with you, you'd accuse me of wanting your inheritance." His words were as sharp as tacks. "So how come you'll accept that from Jason but not from me?"

Laura had backed up against the door, her hands at her throat, as his words pounded images into her brain. The two of them, married, making a home together, a life. Children. Children with his crooked smile and outspoken ways would be a formidable handful. Her breath wheezed in as she suppressed the thought. He was speaking hypothetically. He wasn't proposing.

"I'll tell you why, Laura," he went on, stalking her across the porch. "Because there's more to it than marriage. You're willing to marry a jerk like this Creed because he can give you other things you want—prestige, a place in society."

"That's not true!"

"I think it is. You see, Belle used to read me your letters. You seem to love glamour and glitter, the high-profile, self-serving life you can have with an ambitious man. I'm not like that, Laura. I had that life and it was a sham. *I* was a sham. Now I'm a kennel owner, a member of a small community, building the kind of life you wouldn't be willing to share."

She threw her hands into the air. "If you'll just let me talk...!"

"Oh, save it!" he shouted, and turned to plunge down the steps, his feet crunching gravel as he stormed away.

Laura took one bounding leap after him, then stopped abruptly. She wrapped both hands around a porch post and stood there, watching his moonlit figure disappear into his house. Shaking, she turned and went through her own front door, pushing it shut behind her and staggering to the staircase. She sank down on a step and dropped her forehead against her knuckles.

Devastated, she tried to sift through all he had said. Was he right? Was she more interested in glamour than substance? She tried to recall what had first attracted her to Jason and realized it was his ambition. The first thing she had admired about Sam was his stubborn integrity.

What was Sam offering as an alternative to the life she knew, though? He hadn't said he wanted to marry her or even that he loved her. His whole speech on the subject had been rooted in anger and contempt for her motives.

In her distress, Laura dropped her hands to her lap and gathered up fistfuls of eyelet fabric. She tugged on it as her face crumpled and tears formed. All her fine resolve to stay away from him had done no good. Her stupid deception had been just that—stupid—because she had only deceived herself. From the very first moment, Sam Calhoun had begun changing her life and there was no going back.

She was in love with him.

LAURA DIDN'T SEE Sam for days. It was as if he'd vanished. There were no unexpected appearances at her door. He didn't march over to inform her of new improvements he planned for her house. The bank called to let her know that a large deposit had been made to her checking account. She did some calculations and realized it was enough to last her, and the cats, for the rest of the summer. Did he intend to ignore her for that long? She couldn't say which distressed her more—seeing him or not seeing him.

She found consolation in the cats, who listened without judging her as she talked about the mess she had made. There was plenty to keep her mind occupied. She worked her way through all the papers in her aunt's office, discarding most of them. She saved only the essential documents, including the various community-service awards Belle had won, and the things pertaining to family history.

At last she felt ready to tackle the attic, but after three days of work, she'd barely made a dent. She carefully packed the tea set she and Belle had used so often in their impromptu parties, hoping she would have a little girl of her own someday who would like to do the same thing. When the little girl's image that formed in her mind turned out to have a crooked smile and sable-brown hair, Laura pushed the thought ruthlessly away.

Sam's tirade had accomplished one thing. Whatever else happened, she knew she couldn't

marry Jason. She had fooled herself into
thinking that mutual interests were the same
thing as love. They weren't, and they certainly
weren't enough on which to build a life.

She sat on a rickety imitation Duncan Phyfe
chair, tiredly opening yet another box of Belle's
mementos. Her interest perked up when she
saw that it contained printed programs from
plays Belle had attended in Charleston. Pressed
between the pages were faded and dried cor-
sages with tatters of ribbon still clinging to
them.

Charmed, Laura set these aside, her mind
forming a new image of Belle, that of a femme
fatale with a string of ardent suitors. Next she
found a packet of six letters. They were tied
together with blue ribbon, and Laura knew
they must have been written by someone very
special.

She leaned back in the creaky chair as her
fingers curled around them lightly but possessively. Belle's love letters. A vague memory
stirred, then sprang to life as she recalled a
long-ago conversation concerning Belle's
handsome prince, who had married someone
else.

Laura wondered if these letters were from
him. She set them down hastily, feeling like an
intruder, but her curiosity won out, and she

snatched them up again, disturbing dust that tickled her nose. A mighty sneeze racked her. She dabbed at her eyes and nose with a handkerchief.

With a shake of her head, she wondered if her aunt would mind if she read the letters. Some sense of urgency seemed to demand she do so. Bending the envelopes slightly against her hand, she slipped off the ribbon. With careful reverence, she lifted the flap of the first envelope. The stationery was frail and much creased, but she spread it on her knee and smoothed it out to read words written more than half a century earlier, at the end of the Great Depression.

The writer was witty and warm, and Laura could see immediately why Belle had loved him. He wrote of the classes he was taking at one of the state universities and his job as night janitor and watchman in a tobacco shed. He declared his deep regard for Belle and his eagerness to see her again. Laura smiled at his phrasing.

The other letters continued in much the same vein, the last one ending with his promise to see her when he made a short visit home to Webster during the summer. All the letters were signed with an ornate intertwining of his initials, R.P.

Laura folded them carefully back into their envelopes and slipped on the ribbon. She set them aside and sat quietly pondering them. He had obviously felt deep affection for Belle, had been eager to see her. What happened? Why was there no more correspondence, no more courtship? Laura vaguely remembered Belle's saying she had done something silly and her prince had left. She wondered what it could have been but would probably never know since she didn't even know the man's name. It was possible that he was still alive with a family who might be embarrassed to learn his past, though there was certainly nothing scandalous in his letters to Belle.

With a sad sigh for her beloved aunt's ill-fated love, Laura put the letters with the things to be tossed out. She certainly wouldn't pursue the man's identity. It was history.

Again, she dug into the box at her feet and pulled out a photo album. It was an old black leather one with cracked binding and curled edges. She opened it eagerly to see black-and-white pictures of Belle and her sister, Laura's own grandmother, Lily. Some were candid shots, but most were stiff, posed studio portraits of the two young women and their parents. Further on, she saw pictures of Lily with a young man, whom the caption identified as Robert. With a thrill, Laura studied his face, realizing this was her grandfather, of whom she had never before seen a picture. He was tall, with smiling eyes and light-colored hair that told her he'd probably had her own strawberry-blond locks. The last page contained pictures of her father as a baby, held in the arms of his proud parents.

Smiling at the family treasure she had found, Laura studied each photo carefully until she reached the end. She didn't know why Belle would have stuck such a vital part of the family record up in the attic, but maybe it had simply become misplaced, easy to do in her aunt's crowded house.

At the back of the worn book, she discovered an envelope, yellowed with age. She opened it to find more photographs and tipped the envelope to slide them out into her hand. Only one emerged. Laura's eyes widened at the unmistakable sight of a young Belle, with bobbed hair and bright smile, wrapped possessively in the arms of a young man. They both faced the camera, Belle looking ecstatically happy, the man more reserved.

With a jolt, Laura realized she was looking into the face of her aunt's handsome prince. A second shock followed when she recognized the man as her own grandfather, Robert Decker.

She stared at the picture for several long moments while its meaning raced through her mind. Finally she opened the letters again and studied the ornate initials at the bottom of each. What she had thought was a P was actually a D. Her hands went limp as she let the sheets of paper drift to her lap and stared down at the floor.

Belle had said she'd done something silly, and another princess had married him. There was no indication of what that could have been. Perhaps Belle's mistake had been introducing Robert to Lily. Maybe they had become embroiled in an argument that they couldn't resolve, and Robert had turned to Lily for solace.

Unless she came across other papers somewhere in the house, Laura realized she would probably never know. Tears sprang to her eyes as she gathered up the letters and stuffed them into the album. She swiped at the tears with her fist, smudging the dust on her cheeks.

Clasping the bulging book to her chest, she lurched to her feet and stumbled from the attic. The more she thought about it, the more upset she became, until her body was shaking with sobs.

She clattered down the stairs, then stood at the bottom landing, distraught, turning in circles, wishing she had someone to talk to about her discovery. She thought of her mother, and her hand hovered over the phone, but she glanced at her watch and realized her mother would still be at her secretarial job.

The only other person she could think of was Sam, who had loved Belle as much as Laura had.

Though blinded by tears, she made it across the two yards and rapped on his door. The tears continued to well up in her eyes. Ordinarily she would never have let him see her like this, but now she didn't give it a thought.

When he opened the door, his expression of mild interest changed into one of profound surprise. His brows shot up and his eyes widened. "Laura. What's wrong?" He pulled her inside and shut the door, then whirled to inspect her. "Are you hurt?"

She shook her head and bent over the album. She was holding it so tightly it dug into the insides of her elbows and knifed into her stomach. The pain and sorrow of her aunt's loss crippled her. "Nuh...no," she finally hiccuped. "I'm not hurt."

"Well, what is it?" Sam reached out to skim his fingers over her face, her shoulders, then down her rigid arms. "What's this?"

"It's a fa...hamily album. I fo...hound it in the attic."

His face was puzzled, but concerned by her distress. Gently he pried the leather-bound book from her clutching fingers. "It's all right, sweetheart. Let me see. I'll take care of it."

Laura surrendered it to him and watched as he turned the pages. She lifted a trembling finger. "That's Belle and Lily, my grandmother. But, look—" she showed him the love letters and the photograph of Belle with Robert "—don't you see?" she asked. "This was all she had of the man she loved."

Sam's face was growing as distressed as hers as he tried to fathom her disjointed words. "You mean...she loved her sister's husband?"

Laura nodded mournfully. "Yes, only it was before Robert married Lily. She had to watch her sister marry the man she herself loved, and then raise their son." Sadly she told him what Belle had said about her silliness making her lose her handsome prince.

Sam pulled her with his arms, making sympathetic sounds as she leaned against him. He rubbed her back comfortingly with one hand and held the album with the other. Then he slowly maneuvered her to his couch and sat her down. Laying the album on an end table, he gave her his full attention, his gray eyes brimming with sympathy and understanding. The next thing she knew, Laura was snuggled in his lap, her head tucked under his chin, her long, bare legs resting on the sofa cushions.

He wrapped his arms around her, holding her tightly, safely. "Why does this upset you so much?" he asked, rubbing his cheek against her hair.

"Because she was so wonderful," Laura whispered as she rested her cheek against him. The steady beat of his heart, so strong and solid, thumped against her ear, reassuring her. "She had so much to give. If things had worked out she could have had a houseful of children. She would have been a wonderful mother."

"Honey, what are you talking about? She was a mother to your father, and if things *had* worked out between her and Robert, your father wouldn't have been born, and you wouldn't be here."

Laura lifted her head and looked at him. She gulped back another sob that had been forming. "I hadn't thought of that."

"It's true. And you know, Belle always said that your father and you were the best things that had ever happened to her."

She blinked and her mouth trembled. "Really?" One last tear squeezed out and he lifted his hand to catch it on the end of his finger, then rubbed it over her velvety skin.

"Really." His gaze dropped to her lips. He smoothed the back of his hand along her jaw, then turned his palm to cup it. "And not having you here, next door, is just about the saddest thing I can think of." His voice had dropped to its lowest register.

Suddenly she realized that he had suffered hurts she couldn't imagine. He understood what Belle had gone through, because he had lost someone he once loved, as well as a business he had built from scratch. Sam Calhoun had more grit and guts than she did. She had whined about losing her plum job in Washington, but what did that matter when she had finally found the man she loved?

"What are you thinking, Laura?" he asked, tilting her chin up.

Her answer was an emotion-choked whisper. "I'm thinking what an exceptional man you are."

He brought his face close to hers so that they looked, golden eyes to gray, straight into each other's souls. "Anything else?"

Laura swallowed. "That I'm glad you lived next door to my aunt and did so many things for her."

Sam moved her chin again, then his own head, so that the fit was perfect, but the barest millimeter away. For the space of several thundering heartbeats, they stared at each other. "Anything else?"

Laura closed her eyes, knowing he could read the truth, feeling the unmistakable tug of desire. "That I love you," she whispered, reaching with her lips for his.

Sam obliged her. Laura sighed contentedly, like a woman who has returned home from a long journey. Soon contentment wasn't enough and she sought a deeper passion. It wasn't long in building.

Laura curled her fingers into the collar of his shirt, feeling the warm skin, the strength of bone and sinew. Beneath her legs, his body was firm, cradling and welcoming her.

At last, he eased her away, his eyes shining into hers with ardor and intimacy, respect and love. "Do you mean it? That you love me?"

She swallowed, still dazed by him, knowing that what she said in the next few minutes would seal her fate. Her gaze darted over his face and saw only eager anticipation. "Yes." Her voice was too soft, so she cleared her throat and said it again, louder, so there would be no doubt, "Yes. I love you, and I have something to tell you." Now was the moment to confess the truth about Jason and herself.

His grin lit up the room. "Ah, Laura, I—"

The phone rang at that instant, and across town, the train whistle she had heard before split the air. Before she knew what was happening, Sam had dumped her onto the sofa cushions and leapt to his feet, cursing roundly.

He dragged his hand through hair she had disheveled with her fingers. "Listen, honey, I've got to go."

The phone shrilled again, and she stared at it hazily. "To answer the phone?"

"No." He began looking around for his keys. "I won't answer it."

"But it's ringing," she pointed out as she watched him throw papers off a low table and upend an ottoman.

"I know. Damn, where are those keys? I've got to go. There's the whistle again."

"You're going to meet the train," she said with the air of someone who has just made a great discovery. Her face fell. "Webster doesn't have a train."

"No. That's the new fire alarm. I'm a volunteer fireman. The phone rings in all our houses when the whistle goes off."

Sam slapped his hand to his jeans pocket and shouted with triumph as he yanked out his keys. Looking up, he saw the dazed expression on her face, her lips swollen by his kisses. He groaned deep in his throat and leaned over to kiss her goodbye. "Don't forget where we left off, okay?"

"Okay." She sat up, a smile trembling on her lips, her eyes shining. "But hurry back."

He stopped with his hand on the knob and looked back over his shoulder. His look was thorough, searing and possessive. "I will."

With that, he was gone. Seconds later, Laura heard him start up the old International truck and scatter gravel as he headed out. With an ecstatic sigh, she jumped up, hugging herself. She loved him. Why had she been afraid of it? She'd been a complete idiot. That was all changed now, though. She loved him and she was sure he felt the same way.

Certain he would come to her when he returned from the fire, she snatched up the album, locked his house and rushed back to her own to get ready for him. She showered quickly, blew her hair into a fluff of curls, applied a little makeup, then dressed in a peasant-style dress she'd had a seamstress make for her in Senegal. It was pale green, with off-the-shoulder sleeves, and had yards of skirt that flirted about her knees, showing them off. She prepared a special dinner and was looking at her watch, trying to decide if she had time to run out for a bottle of wine when the doorbell rang.

On a rush of joy she hurried to the door and hauled it open—to see Jason Creed standing on her porch.

CHAPTER TEN

"HELLO, DARLING. Aren't you going to invite me in?" Jason's smooth greeting barely touched the surface of Laura's shock.

Her eyes were wide, her body stiff. If she hadn't had her hand wrapped around the edge of the door, she probably would have collapsed in a heap. "Jason?"

He stepped forward and slipped an arm around her waist as he bent to kiss her cheek. She managed to dredge up enough presence of mind to duck away so that his mouth glanced off the hair near her ear. His brow furrowed. "Laura, what's wrong?" With his hand at her waist, he urged her inside and shut the door.

Her body felt limp, although her mind was beginning to race, adding up all the complications that could develop from his visit. She couldn't even manage a smile. "I'm just so surprised to see you. Why didn't you tell me you were coming?"

He surveyed the room, taking in the new paint, the piles of things yet to be sorted and dealt with, then swung back to her. "I didn't know myself until almost the day I left. I had to come back to Washington for some policy meetings and decided to take a couple of days off to see you. I flew into Greenville and rented a car."

A wavery smile finally formed on her lips, then died as she inspected him. Jason was the same height as she was, and when they'd gone out together she had always worn flats. His face was handsome in a quiet way. He liked to know exactly what was going on at all times and was an expert on government policies affecting his job. That explained his attendance at the meetings. But something was fishy here. "Jason, why didn't you call first?"

He shrugged. "I wanted to surprise you. Aren't you glad to see me?"

Laura chewed her bottom lip. Jason hated surprises, and she couldn't imagine him springing one on her.

When she didn't answer, he stepped to the entrance of the dining room. His eyes grew round at the sight of the perfectly kept cherrywood suite. "This house is beautiful." He looked back over his shoulder. "What's the real-estate market like around here? Think we'll be able to get a good price for this place?"

"I don't know." Her mind was racing a thousand miles an hour. Sam would be returning any minute, but Jason had arrived uninvited and unwelcomed. She had to get him out of here, but how? And how could she explain that she had been using him as a shield to keep herself from falling for Sam? She took a deep breath to steady herself. "I can't really think about that yet. I have to be here for almost a year yet, you know. Jason," she said desperately, "there's something I have to tell you."

Jason walked back to her and, smiling widely, put his arm around her waist once again. "Of course. Is there someplace we can sit down?"

Holding herself stiffly, Laura led him into the living room and indicated the comfortable old couch. He adjusted the precise creases in his slacks and sat, then looked up curiously when she took a chair opposite him. "Laura, what's wrong?"

Her gaze darted around nervously. "Why don't you tell me what you have to say first?" she said, calling herself every kind of coward.

Discomfort marred his features for just a minute, but he nodded and said gamely, "I was wondering if there was some way this could be settled early and we could get married now."

"Now?" Laura's voice shot up.

"I've realized I don't want to wait for you." His smile was just the least bit unctuous, and she wondered why she had never noticed it before. "If you've become friendly with the man who's executor of your aunt's estate, perhaps we could resolve things right away and get married. You could come back to Senegal with me. We could have a nice house, do some entertaining..."

Friendly? She had become more than friendly with Sam Calhoun. Knowing this, and knowing she had let matters drag on with Jason for too long, she could have kicked herself. She had no one else to blame. Sam had warned her that Jason was only interested in the money, and now the evidence was right before her. There were many forms of foolishness, and one of them was Laura Decker, she thought in dismay.

"Jason, I'm sorry you've come all this way for nothing, but—" The doorbell rang. Laura jerked forward on her chair and sat, frozen, as she stared in the direction of the door. A horrible premonition told her exactly who it was. She didn't know why Sam had chosen this moment to become polite rather than just opening the door and barging in like he usually did, but maybe she should be grateful. She would have a moment with him to try to explain things before he came face-to-face with Jason.

"Laura, aren't you going to answer that?" Jason asked, clearly puzzled by her strange behavior.

"Of... of course." She gave him a vague look, rose to her feet and started for the door, which was mercifully separated from the living room by the entryway.

Her heart pounding, her throat full of dread, she opened the door to see Sam Calhoun standing on her porch. He held an enormous bouquet of flowers that must have been freshly picked from his yard. He wore a tailored blue suit that made him look ruggedly handsome. A bottle of wine was tucked under his arm.

Reaching forward, Sam wrapped his free hand around her and drew her to him. "Hello, honey. You look gorgeous." He kissed her surprised lips, then lifted his head and sniffed the air, redolent with the dinner she had prepared. His eyes shone down at her, warm and laughing wickedly. "I can only hope all this was for me."

"Oh, oh, yes... I..." She couldn't go on. Color washed out of her face, then back in.

Sam came into the house and nudged the door shut with his foot. "The fire was just old Mr. Burton burning trash near a rundown shed. He knows better than that. The dry lumber in the shed went up like a Roman candle. Scared the old coot half to death." When she didn't respond, he frowned, set his flowers and wine on a nearby table and faced her. "There's a car out on the street, and I...Laura?"

"Laura?" Jason called from the living room, then appeared in the doorway.

She didn't even turn, but kept her eyes fixed resolutely on Sam's face. "Sam, this is Jason Creed. He had meetings in Washington, then came down here to, uh, surprise me." Her eyes pleaded with him to understand, to give her the benefit of the doubt. Not that she deserved it.

Jason, oblivious to the undercurrents between her and Sam, hurried forward to pump Sam's hand. "Glad to meet you, Calhoun. This is an opportune time for you to stop in."

That's what he thinks!, Laura looked at Jason wildly, then back at Sam, whose face had gone from loving and friendly to suspicious and austere. Granite chips could have been struck from his jaw.

"Yeah," he growled. "It looks like an auspicious time."

"We were wondering if there is some way you could expedite the matter of Laura's aunt's will." He slipped an arm around her frozen shoulders. "We want to get married as soon as possible."

"Oh, is that right?"

An astute man would have been wary of a tone that sounded like a rattlesnake just before it strikes, but Jason seemed to have lost the intelligence with which Laura had always credited him. "Yes. We simply can't wait any longer."

"Is this true, Laura?" Sam's attention swung to her. If his eyes had been lasers, she would be nothing but smoking remains right now.

She licked her lips. "No. Not exactly. Listen, Sam," she said, near hysteria, "I've got to explain—"

His formidable brows lifted and his chin jutted forward. "Don't bother. And think about this—I only have control of the late Miss McCord's trust account which holds enough money for Laura's expenses for the rest of the year and no more. The bulk of the estate is tied up in probate and will be for several months. I can't hurry the process. It's state law. You'll just have to wait." With that and a contemptuous glance in Laura's direction, he turned, wrenched the door open and headed out into the twilight.

Appalled, Laura twisted from Jason's embrace and rushed after Sam. She caught up with him at the corner of the house. "Sam, wait! I've made a mess of things, but this isn't what you think—"

"And just what do I think, Laura?" he asked, turning back to her, his face full of rage, his shoulders stiff. "Do I think you used me? Yes. Do I think you're the money-hungry brat I've always thought you were? Yes."

Her hands formed into fists as she forgot about the explanations tumbling about in her mind and became suddenly, righteously, angry. "I had no idea Jason was coming," she said, her voice rising. "And I certainly didn't use you in any way. I don't expect you to believe that. You're an expert at jumping to conclusions about me. You did it long before we even met." Her full skirt swirled like a matador's cape and she ran back to her house. Half of her wanted to hear him calling out to her; the other half wanted to throw something heavy at him if he did. There was no sound, though, so she dashed up her stairs and into the house to face Jason.

He looked taken aback by the wild-eyed woman who burst through the front door.

She stalked up to him. "Exactly why do you want the money from my aunt's estate so badly, Jason?"

"Why, I—"

"Let me tell you something that might just change your mind." She slapped her hands onto her hips as she faced him. "I have no intention of using that money for myself. I have to take care of Aunt Belle's cats. Other than that, I won't touch a penny. The bulk of the estate will go home."

His Adam's apple bobbed. "Home?"

"To Alaska. To educate my younger brothers and sisters, especially Amy and Todd. They're going to be doctors—great doctors— and I'm going to pay for their education with my inheritance. You see, I'm not interested in money, Jason." She held out her hands. "I've got these to earn a living with. I've got a mind and a lot of determination. Why is it that *you* want the money?"

Jason's face had hardened. "You could have told me all this earlier. You could have written or called. You misled Calhoun and me."

Shame reddened her face. "Yes, I did, and I'm sorry, but you didn't answer my question."

"About why I'm anxious for your inheritance to come through?" He lifted his elegant shoulders. "It's very simple. I'm damned sick and tired of living within my means. I want to live rich. Be rich.''

Her lips thinned. ''You want money and prestige.''

''Don't condemn me, Laura,'' he said, his voice tight. ''You wanted the prestige of your career.''

''That's true,'' she acknowledged with a nod. ''But I see now that there are more important things. Things I had forgotten for a while.''

He moved past her. ''I might as well go. You've got your mind made up.''

She nodded sadly. ''A marriage between us wouldn't have worked, Jason. We would both have been miserable because we don't love each other. Without love there's no incentive to overcome problems.''

He watched her for a long moment before he opened the door. His glance took in the darkening sky. ''I don't have to guess who you do love, do I?'' He smiled but it didn't reach his eyes.

''No, you don't.'' Not that it was going to do her any good to love Sam. He'd probably never speak to her again.

Without saying goodbye, Jason walked out of her life. Laura leaned against the doorjamb, watching him go and feeling sorrow at the loss of a friend. They had been two different people in Paris and Dakar. She had been irreparably changed by moving next door to Sam Calhoun.

Her gaze drifted to Sam's house, where a light shone in the living room, piercing the lonely darkness. Hurt, still angry, Laura dashed back into her house and shut out the night.

In a daze, she went into the kitchen and turned off the oven. She didn't bother to remove the casserole she had placed inside. What was the point? She couldn't imagine ever being hungry again.

Why couldn't Sam believe her? Why did he automatically think the worst? Because of his past marriage? Probably, but he should be able to realize she wasn't like his ex-wife, Myra, or whatever her name was. So it must be that he didn't really love her, then, or he would have waited for an explanation.

As had become her habit, she sought out the cats for comfort. "Oh, Aunt Belle," she murmured, stumbling toward the sun-room, "I've made a mess of things, and your friend, Sam, hasn't helped a bit!"

She swept into the room, expecting to be greeted by a swift rush of affection. Instead she heard a low, distressed groan. Alarmed, she flipped on the lights to see Guinevere stretched across one of the window seats, obviously in pain. Her head was angled back, her eyes slitted.

Laura knelt beside her, touching her thick fur, but the cat ignored her. Leaping up, she hurried to find the veterinarian's phone number, then cursed when his answering service said he was on vacation, and had referred his cases to a colleague in the next town.

Without even considering, Laura plunked the receiver down and dashed from her house to Sam's. She knew she should have had more pride, but as she raced across the lawn, she reminded herself that her silly pride had caused nothing but disaster.

She didn't even have to knock because he was there, his suit jacket off, his tie loosened, a glass of some amber-colored liquid in his hand. He stared at her in surprise.

"I saw lover boy leaving," he said, eyeing her. "I was just thinking about coming over to—"

"Sam, please help me. There's something wrong with Guinevere." She grasped his arm and pulled him after her. He barely had time to set down his drink and shut his front door before she had him down the steps and across the yard.

Once they were in the sun-room, he hurried to examine the cat. He ran his hand over her and went still, then looked up at Laura's anxious face. His crooked grin came into play.

Laura gaped at him. "Why are you smiling? She's in pain! Do something!"

He chuckled. "Don't worry. It's just nature taking its course." He sat back on his heels. "She's having kittens."

If he had produced a hammer and bounced it off her forehead, she couldn't have been more stunned. "Kittens? But she's too old. The vet said she was too old to spay."

"Vets have been wrong before. Mother Nature works in mysterious ways." He waggled a finger at her. "Let this be a lesson to you. Watch the cats when you let them outside. There are others in the neighborhood, you know, who haven't been neutered."

She held up her hand and ticked backward on her fingers as she recalled the length of a cat's gestation period. "Now wait a minute. This happened before I came! Obviously, my aunt let her pets out once in a while when you didn't know about it."

He shrugged as if it was of no importance. "Maybe. Why don't you get her a cardboard box and an old towel or blanket? We can make her comfortable."

Laura got an empty box from Belle's old office and lined it with some worn towels. They set it in a corner of the kitchen and Sam carefully placed the expectant mother inside. When she was settled, he turned and looked at Laura.

"You had no idea she was pregnant?"

"No. The only times I've ever been around cats was when I visited here. We had dogs at home and..." She shook her head helplessly. "Well, I just thought Guinevere was getting fat."

"She'll be thin again pretty soon," he said dryly. "Why don't we get out of here and give her some peace? She's an old pro at this. She doesn't need us."

Laura nodded and led him to the entryway, expecting him to leave. Instead he went on into the living room. Curious, she followed. He stood and looked around, his hands on his hips.

"Lover boy gone to get a motel room?" His incredible lashes opened wide over guileless gray eyes.

Laura watched him warily, noting the anger and hurt that had hardened his face before was gone. She felt her distress fading, allowing hope to rush in. "He's gone permanently. I told him I have no intention..." She looked at him significantly. "Never had any intention of keeping my inheritance for myself. As soon as I learned about it, I decided to use it to educate the younger kids in my family, especially my brother and sister who want to be doctors.''

She saw respect flicker on his face as he asked, "And Jason didn't like that idea?''

"He didn't like that idea.'' She met his look with a challenge of her own—chin up, eyes direct. "Sam, this whole misunderstanding between you and me is my fault. I had thought about marrying Jason because we seemed to have so much in common, but we'd never really made it a official. Then when I came here, everything moved so fast and you were so...overwhelming that it was easier to let you think I was going to marry Jason.'' She bit her lip, frowning. "It seemed as if I could never get things straightened out. I'm sorry. I was wrong. I was also wrong to ever think I could marry Jason. I don't love him.''

Sam faced her fully, then took a step forward. His eyes began to gleam. "Is that right?''

Excitement, happiness, began to grow in her. "That's right.'' She moved closer to him.

"I take it you love someone else?'' Sam reached her and they stood toe-to-toe, his clothes barely brushing hers, his hands at his sides.

"You take it right."

"May I ask who?"

Laura's hands shook as she lifted them. Hesitantly she placed them on his chest. His heart rumbled beneath her fingertips. Her eyes were drenched with her feelings as she looked at him. "I already told you."

"Tell me again."

"You tell me first."

"This isn't a game." His throat worked. His lips were pinched, as though he was trying to keep his emotions from spilling out.

"I never thought it was. I'm deadly serious." Her hands trembled against the crisp cloth of his shirt.

His arms closed around her, and his lips moved against her fragrant hair. "I love you, Laura. I have since Belle started reading me your letters. I was hooked by your brains and ambition, your sense of humor, but I thought I'd made another bad choice of a woman to love when you didn't come to see Belle. You seemed to ignore her needs.

"Once you were here, though, you started working your way into my life, into my thoughts. I couldn't believe you were going to marry that pompous ass. It made me furious, but still, I loved you. I figured if I had a year, I could convince you to love me. When you found that picture and came running over, I knew I didn't have to wait any longer." His arms tightened. "Then tonight, seeing Creed here, I thought you had used me, and I swore I would never again be used by a woman who's interested only in money." His voice lowered. "I was wrong. I was jealous. You're everything I want."

Tears shimmered in her eyes. "I love you, Sam. I'm sorry about Jason. I should never have let myself drift into that situation—or deceived you about it. You were right. He was only interested in my inheritance. When he found out I was going to use the money for my family, he lit out of here like a scalded cat." Her eyes widened as a thought struck. "Cat!"

"What's the matter?"

"The will said I had to take care of Belle's cats until they, or their issue, died!" Laughing near hysteria, she collapsed into Sam's arms. "Guinevere's having kittens. I'll be taking care of cats for the rest of my life!"

Sam caught her, laughing with her, spreading kisses over her bright hair, her flushed face. "Then you'd better marry me. We're going to need both pieces of property for all the cats, dogs and kids we're going to have."

Her eyes full of love, she tilted her head back to look up at him. "Oh, yes, Sam," she breathed. "I'll marry you." She slipped her arms around his neck, enjoying the sensations only he could arouse in her. Laura smiled against his mouth. This was home, where she belonged.

THEIR WEDDING two months later seemed to have a cast of thousands. Sam's family was there in full force, and so was Laura's. Not to be outdone, the town of Webster had attended en masse. Laura looked around during the reception and was convinced that every house in town must be deserted.

She was delighted to meet Sam's mother and sisters. She suspected that Will and Bret, who had been groomsmen, were making moves on her sisters, Amy and Sarah, but she knew the two girls could hold their own. The younger members of their families seemed to be forming fast friendships. Her own mother and stepfather were dancing dreamily to the music provided by a local country band.

"What are you thinking about?" Sam asked, placing a kiss aimlessly on her white tulle veil as their feet moved together to the music.

She turned her shining gaze up to him. "How happy I am. How lucky that Belle made her will as she did."

Sam chuckled, his craggy face content. "I have the feeling luck had little to do with it."

"What do you mean?"

"Oh, Mrs. Calhoun." Mr. Pine's voice spoke from behind them.

Feeling a thrill at being called by that name, Laura turned and smiled. "Yes?"

The little man bowed in a courtly manner and said, "I want to offer you my congratulations and best wishes."

Laura exchanged a sparkling glance with her new husband. "Thank you."

Mr. Pine's lips flickered in a smile as he pulled an envelope from his pocket. "I was also instructed to give you this on the occasion of your wedding."

"What is it?" Laura asked, accepting it.

"Read it and find out." He disappeared into the crush of guests.

Laura's eyes filled with tears as she looked down and recognized Belle's handwriting on an envelope addressed to Mr. and Mrs. Sam Calhoun. "What on earth...?" Quickly she slipped a nail under the flap and extracted a short note.

Sam read over her shoulder and they both burst out laughing when they reached the end.

Laura's husband swept her into his arms, and much to the delight of the wedding guests, kissed her thoroughly. "That's what I meant about it not being luck."

Laura shook her head in wonder and gratitude as she looked at the note again.

"My darling Laura, I kept my promise," it read. "Here's your handsome prince. I love you both. Belle."

Take 4 bestselling love stories FREE

Plus get a FREE surprise gift!